FAERIEGROUND

Wish

by beth bracken & kay fraser

illustrated by odessa sawyer

capstone young readers

FAERIEGROUND IS PUBLISHED BY
CAPSTONE YOUNG READERS
A CAPSTONE IMPRINT
1710 ROE CREST DRIVE
NORTH MANKATO, MINNESOTA 56003
WWW.CAPSTONEYOUNGREADERS.COM

LIBRARY OF CONGRESS CATALOGING-IN-PUBLICATION DATA IS
AVAILABLE ON THE LIBRARY OF CONGRESS WEBSITE.

ISBN: 978-1-62370-003-4
SUMMARY: SOLI AND LUCY ARE BEST FRIENDS—UNTIL, ON
FAERIEGROUND, SOLI WISHES LUCY AWAY.

THIS BOOK IS ALSO AVAILABLE AS FOUR LIBRARY-BOUND
EDITIONS:

A WISH IN THE WOODS 978-1-4342-3303-5
THE SHADOWS 978-1-4342-3306-6
BLOODFATE 978-1-4342-3305-9
THE WILLOW QUEEN'S GATE 978-1-4342-3304-2

BOOK DESIGN BY K. FRASER
ALL PHOTOS © SHUTTERSTOCK WITH THESE EXCEPTIONS:
AUTHOR PORTRAIT © K FRASER
ILLUSTRATOR PORTRAIT © ODESSA SAWYER

PRINTED IN CHINA
042013
007289R

> *"Wishes come true, not free."*
> – Stephen Sondheim, Into the Woods

For Valarie, who wished me away, and wished me home. -b
For the Fraser sisters; you are all a mother could wish for. -k

Long ago, a kingdom was founded in Willow Forest . . .

The faerieground and human village weren't far from each other. They shared a dark wood. They shared the same sun, water, trees, and air. Visitors crossed the borders.

They were happy neighbors. At first.

In the village, unrest was growing.

And in the faerieground, nothing was quite what it seemed.

Over time, the human village and the faerie kingdom grew further apart. Some humans began to spread rumors that the faeries were evil. Some faeries believed that the humans were murderers. The balance shifted. Things were changing.

And then there was a new queen of the faeries.

Calandra.

The kingdom welcomed Calandra as their queen. The king deserved love and happiness. He was a good faerie, maybe one of the best. The wedding was beautiful. It was a time of goodwill and joy. The kingdom rejoiced.

Then tragedy happened. The faerie kingdom fell quickly into ruin. Only one thing could fix it.

One wish.

The faerieground is still
there, just past a wish made
in the woods . . .

Part 1

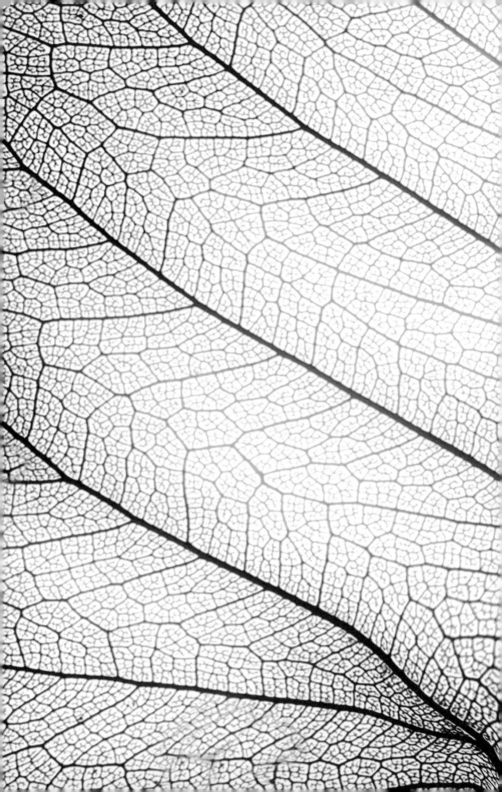

1

Soli

We are always together, Lucy and I.

Lucy is the brave one.
I am the fearful one.

We were born two weeks apart in different towns, but since then, we've always been together.

We are the kind of friends everyone wants.
We are never apart.

Her mother may as well be my mother.

I spend hours at her house.

Lucy knows everything about me.

Every detail of my life.

And I know absolutely everything about her.

We are best friends. We do everything together. We always have.

Or we did, anyway.

We used to.

Before.

We live in Mearston, a small town on the edge of Willow Forest. The trees in the woods are as old as trees can be. It's dark in there, dark and scary and beautiful.

Everyone says to stay out of the woods.

Lucy's mother told her the woods were called the faerieground. She told us never to go there. She said that faeries lived there.

She said if you made a wish in the woods, your wish would come true.

That you'd wish you hadn't wished it.

We started going there when we were little girls, Lucy and I. We were five or six, roaming around on our own.

I didn't want to go in. But Lucy said, "This will be our secret shortcut." It made our walk to school half as long. So we had extra time to play, to talk, to laugh, to be together.

Lucy is not afraid of the woods. So neither am I.
Not anymore.

But I'm careful there. I stay behind her. That's what best friends do. They stay together.

Now we are thirteen.

I still stay behind her.

Lucy has always led the way.

She does everything first.

She was born first.

Our mothers tell us she walked first, talked first.

Her first word was *sky*.

Mine was *Lucy*.

She kissed a boy first. Last week.

I wouldn't care. I'd be happy for her. I'm used to her doing things first. I'm used to just being happy for her. Except for one thing.

It was Jaleel.

He's the boy I like.

Jaleel is strong. He's smart. His smile is amazing, especially when he smiles at me. It's like I know a secret about him that no one in the world could guess. It's like we know something secret about each other.

At school, I stay in shadowy corners, in dark spaces. Lucy is out in the light. She's popular and friendly and bold.

I am shy and quiet. Hardly anyone knows me, besides Lucy. I've never bothered to try to get anyone else to know me.

I never thought I'd need another friend, not really. Not when I had Lucy.

When she's around, she puts everyone in the shadows. And I never mind.

That's just who we are.
Two sides of the same coin.
Two halves of the same whole.

She makes the light, and I stay in the dark.

But somehow, Jaleel saw me in the shadows.

Lucy knew I liked him, and she kissed him anyway.

Then she told me about it.

She said she was sorry.

She said it just happened.

She said it wouldn't happen again.

Of course, I believed her.

I thought I would forgive her.

I thought she was my best friend, and she'd never lie to me.

Then at school today, I saw them together.

I was walking through the crowds after lunch, looking for Lucy. She was at her locker, fixing her long, blond hair.

She's beautiful. Have I mentioned that?

Lucy is beautiful. I have always thought that she was more beautiful than me. But the thing about her is that you don't notice her beauty, because she's so kind, too.

She's not one of those girls who is just pretty and nothing else.
She's different.

Anyway. She was at her locker. Her hair looked perfect. The crowds parted.

I smiled and waved, but Lucy didn't see me. She wasn't looking my way. She was smiling up at someone else, someone taller.

And the crowds parted more, and as everyone moved from between us I could see who the someone else was.

It was Jaleel.

He leaned down and kissed her. She stood up on her tiptoes, reaching for him.

That's when Lucy saw me.

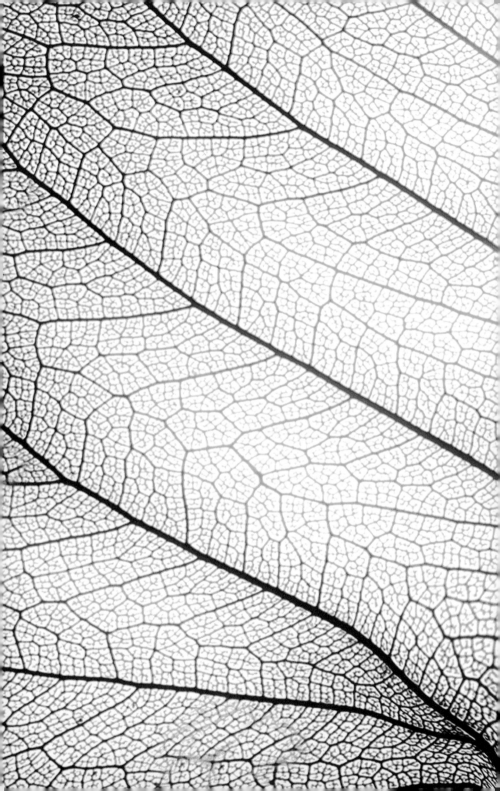

Lucy

Soli is like my sister.

All I want is to take care of her and make her happy.
She spends so much time feeling bad, feeling dark, hiding
away from everyone.

I wish she'd come out in the light like me. I wish she'd
let people see how wonderful she is. I wish she could do
that.

I love Soli. Like a sister. Except she's not my sister.
And here's the thing: Sometimes I think my mother likes
Soli more than she likes me.

I know that's crazy. But ever since we were born, Soli has spent hours and hours and hours at my house.

I've watched them together.

My mother has fed her. My mother has bought her clothes. My mother has dried her tears. And my mother watches her.

Not in a creepy way. In a loving way. In a careful way. In a protective way. In a way she hardly ever looks at me.

As if Soli needs extra care. As if her own mother is not enough. As if my mother needs to take care of her too.

Or like I don't deserve as much care.

Sometimes I feel like I've left Soli behind. Sometimes it feels like she doesn't like doing the things I do. She's so quiet. She's so careful. I like being loud and bright and full of life.

Once I had a party. I was ten. My mother bought cake and sparklers.

I didn't invite Soli. I didn't even tell her about it.

When my mother found out, she cried. "She's your best friend," my mother said.

She is. She is my best friend. She is like the other half of me.

So of course I changed my mind. I invited Soli to the party.

But is there anything wrong with wanting something that could be just mine? Something I wouldn't have to share with my best friend, my sister?

My own mother? My own friends? My own party? My own boyfriend?

Does it make me a bad person?

She asked me to talk to Jaleel and I did. I talked to him. And I liked him. I didn't mean to. It just happened. Sometimes when you talk to someone, it just happens. You like them. And we kissed, and I told Soli about it, and I said I was sorry and that it would never happen again.

I thought it was true.

Then, at school today, she saw me kiss him again.

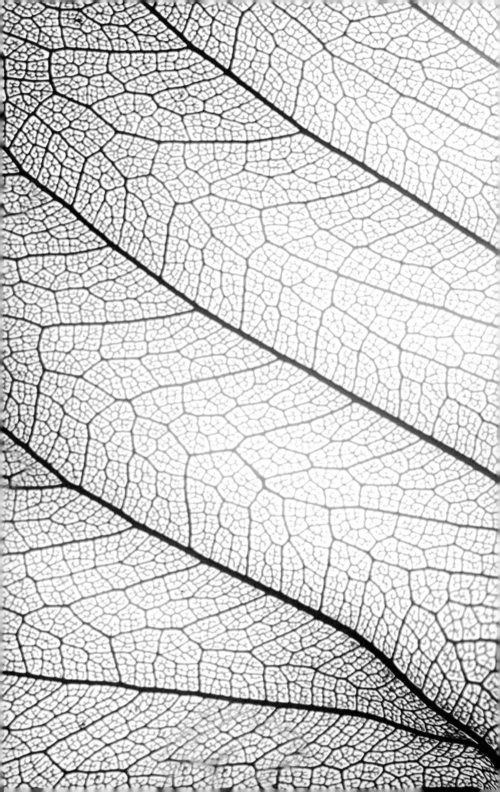

Soli

After school, I run home through our shortcut in the woods. I follow the path I know so well. I've never traveled it alone.

My backpack bounces against my back and my heart pounds. My feet stamp the ground.

I hear her voice. "Soli!" she calls. "Soledad! Wait! Stop, Soli, stop!"

I don't want to stop.

So I keep going.

Right now, I feel like I never want to talk to Lucy ever
again.

"Come on, Soli, wait up," she calls. "I mean it. Turn
around! Let me talk to you. Please! Soli, please!"

In my head, I'm thinking *No, no, no.*

But my legs stop moving.

I stand in the middle of Willow Forest, waiting for
Lucy to catch up to me.

She grabs my hands, and I pull them away.

She looks me in the eye, and I turn my face.

"Why did you lie to me?" I ask.

Lucy sits down on the grass.

"I didn't mean to," she says. She pulls out stems of clovers and twists them in her long fingers. "I meant it when I said it wouldn't happen again. I didn't think he actually liked me."

"Maybe he doesn't," I say.

I want to hurt her feelings. I want to make her feel as bad, as stupid, as pathetic as she's made me feel.

How has this happened to us?

How can I have these feelings of anger toward my best friend?

Lucy shrugs. "Maybe not," she tells me. "Maybe he doesn't really like me."

Then she looks up at me.

She stands and pushes a string of flyaway hair away from my face. "Maybe he doesn't like me," she repeats.

"Maybe," I whisper.

Lucy looks away.

"But now," she says. "Now I think I really like him. I'm sorry."

I feel tears crawling out of my eyes. One slips down my face.

"How could you do that to me?" I ask.

"I know you like him," Lucy says softly. "And I know why."

"Why?" I ask.

"Because he's a nice guy," Lucy says. "Because he's nice to you. Because he notices you."

She's right about that.

Jaleel notices me.

And not in a bad way, either.

And he is nice to me, nicer than any other boy I've ever known.

Once I was in the hallway and I tripped. I don't know how it happened.

Maybe my shoe came untied.
Maybe someone stuck their foot out on purpose.
Maybe I just fell.

Oh, it was so embarrassing.

Sprawled on the floor, I felt my cheeks getting hot.
I'm not used to people looking at me. Everyone saw.
Everyone started to laugh.

Not Jaleel.

He reached down and helped me up. Then he smiled at me and walked away.

Lucy would have helped me. But she wasn't there.
And now that I think about it, maybe she would have laughed too.

Now she sits in the woods, trying to apologize. Trying to say she's sorry for liking a boy who's likable.

I should be able to understand.

After all, I liked him first.

But she promised. She said she'd go to the game, that she'd talk to him.

I couldn't go.

If I'd gone, would things be different?

Would he be kissing me in the hall?

Would Lucy be the jealous one?

Maybe.

But she wouldn't be the hurt one.

She wouldn't be the betrayed one.

She has never hurt me like this before.

"I understand that you're mad," she says. "But—"

"No," I say.

I shake my head.

Lucy

Sometimes you hurt your friends.

Sometimes you make your mother mad. Sometimes you have to.

I guess today was my turn to hurt the person I love most in the world.

As soon as it happened, everything turned dark inside me. As soon as I saw Soli's dark eyes. I felt strange. I felt horrible. I felt like a burned bowl of rose petals. I felt ruined.

I knew if I could take it back, I would. I know I would.

When I chased her into the forest, I was also chasing myself. The good Lucy. Light Lucy. Lucy who makes her mother proud. Lucy who makes a mistake but fixes it.

When I finally invited Soli to the birthday party, the one I didn't want to tell her about, her eyes lit up. She didn't know everyone else had already been invited.

"It'll be so much fun!" she said.

I remember still, years later, exactly how her face looked. Full of hope. Full of trust. She wasn't surprised to be invited. She knew she belonged there.

And I felt terrible. I should have invited her first. I wasn't sure why I hadn't. I'm still not sure.

Sometimes friends start to feel like they aren't friends. Sisters feel like strangers.

Or maybe it was me who was changing.

After that, I was afraid to ever let Soli out of my sight. I didn't want to make my mother angry. And I was afraid of who I'd be without my other half.

Now, in the woods, Soli is angry with me. She should be. I kissed the boy she likes. I lied to her.

It's like the birthday party, except this time she found

out, and I didn't have time to fix it. I couldn't make it all go away. I couldn't un-kiss Jaleel, and I'm not sure I would if I could.

"I understand that you're mad," I say, sitting back down on the ground, pulling clovers, counting leaves. "But—"

"No," Soli says.

We have been friends for thirteen years. We will be friends for many more. She'll forgive me. I know she will.

Inside I feel my light coming back.

Like the sun is rising.

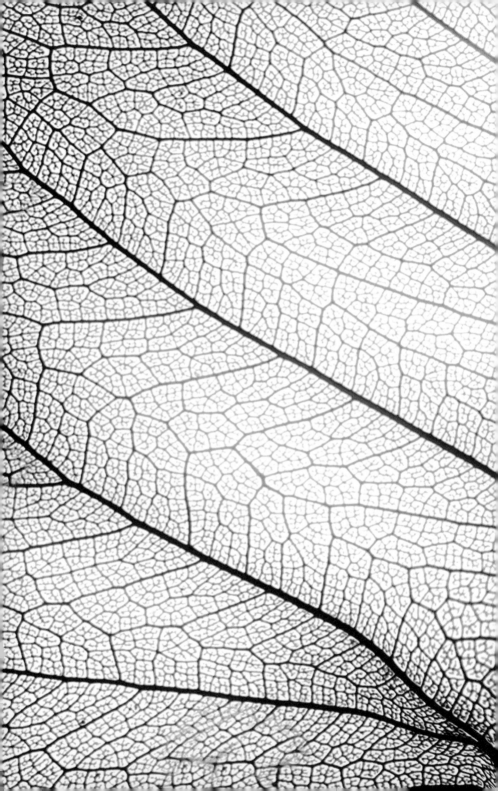

4

Soli

It started when Jaleel and I walked home together.

A few days ago. Lucy was sick. I left school and took the long way home.

Soon I heard footsteps behind me.

"Wait up, Soli!" a voice said.

It was Jaleel, and he wanted to walk with me. And yes, I wanted to walk with him too.

We talked about math class.

We talked about how the leaves crunch under your feet in the fall.

We talked about my dog and how he barks at thunder.

I am not good at talking to people.

But I was good at talking to Jaleel.

Jaleel laughed every time I made a joke. I made more jokes. We talked. We looked at each other and smiled. Sometimes we were quiet, but it didn't make me feel scared.

At a corner not far from my house, he stopped. "This is my street," he told me. "See you tomorrow."

"Okay," I said. "See you tomorrow." And I smiled, and I felt my face light up.

I went home feeling like I was holding a red-hot rose in my heart.

The next day I walked to school alone, the long way. I lingered by Jaleel's street, hoping he'd find me. He finally jogged down the block just as I was about to leave.

"Hey, Soli!" he said, slowing to a stop. "I'm so happy to see you."

"You are?" I asked.

Then I smiled. "I'm happy to see you too," I said.

We walked to school together. We talked the whole time.

When we were separating to walk to class, Jaleel asked if I was going to the basketball game.

"I hope you do," he said. "You should. You should come."

"I don't think I can," I told him.

I'd promised to help my mom with something.

I don't remember what.

But I knew I couldn't get out of it.

Not for a basketball game.

I tried to hold tight to the rose in my chest.

He wanted me to go to the game.

That was enough for now.

After school, I walked home through the woods with Lucy.

I told her everything. All about Jaleel. I'd never really liked a boy before. She knew that.

She knew that.

She didn't know his name, but she knew who he was when I described him, his dark hair, his long legs, his smile, his eyes.

"I'm going to the game," she told me. "I'll talk to him. See if he says anything about you. Don't worry. I'll make this happen."

I waited all night. Just the sight of the phone made my heart grow.

She finally called, late.

She'd been at the game.
She sat by Jaleel.
They talked.

She mentioned me, and he said I was cool.

My heart heated up.

Then she stopped talking for a minute.
There was more to the story.

After the game, while she waited for her dad to pick her up, Jaleel had kissed her.

Or she had kissed him. She didn't know.

Her voice shook as she told me.

"It was a total accident," she told me. "It didn't mean anything. I think he might like you!"

When I saw them in the hall today, the rose in my chest turned to coal.

Soli

In the woods, I stare at Lucy.

"No," I say again.

"You're not mad?" Lucy asks, her face full of hope. "Oh, good!"

"No," I say. "I am mad. I'm really mad. Right now I just wish you weren't here."

A bright light bursts in the darkness of the forest. It blinds me.

Then there's silence.

Just like that, Lucy is gone.

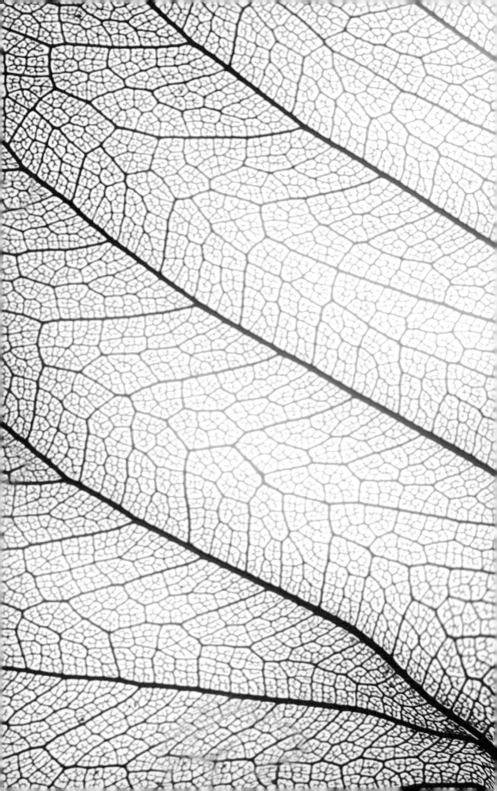

5

Lucy

In the woods, Soli was angry.

I would have been angry too.

Wouldn't you? Your best friend kisses the boy you think you like—how would you feel? And imagine you're the friend who does the kissing. How would that feel? Who feels worse, the betrayed or the betrayer?

I feel like the worst friend ever.

I didn't mean to like him. I meant to get him to like Soli. When she talked about him, her face lit up.

Soli likes to be in the shadows. Jaleel made her feel light.

I wanted him to feel like that about her. But talking to him, and kissing him, his lips pressed against mine—that made me feel light as air and twice as bright. I forgot about Soli.

Would Soli have forgotten about me?

If it was the other way around. What would she have done?

Would she have kissed him back?

In the woods, when she was angry, Soli made a wish.

As long as Soli and I have been coming to the woods, I've been trying to keep her from wishing. The woods can't hurt you if you don't wish. Anyone who believes in faeries knows that.

I don't know for sure if I believe in them. But I never let Soli believe in them, in the faeries. That was the one thing I did to keep her safe. My one protection. I told her my mother's stories were just that. Stories. After all, I wasn't sure. For all I knew they could just be stories my mother told me. Fairytales.

Soli's mother wasn't from here. She had no reason to believe. Her mother hadn't heard the stories her whole life. Not like my mother.

The faeries, if they're here, they've kept their distance. It hasn't been easy. And if Soli ever said, "I wish—" I would change the subject or interrupt her.

This time I didn't stop her.

And she wished me away.

Away to the faerieground.

Part 2

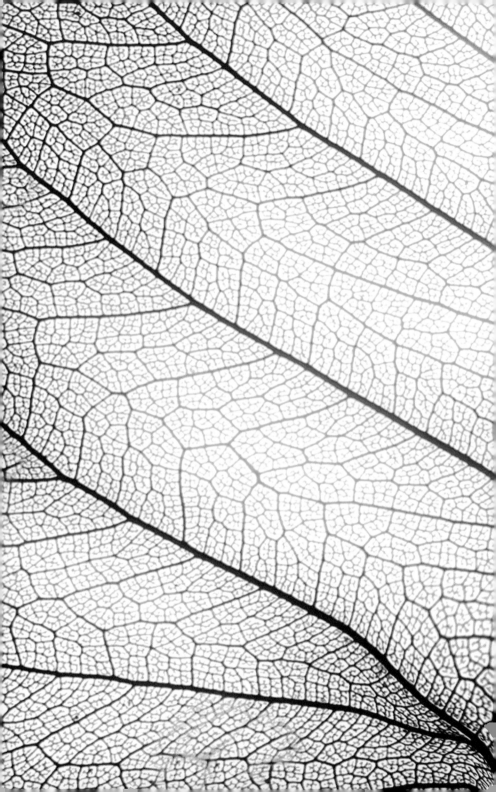

Lucy

The faeries aren't at all how I imagined them. I thought they'd be pretty, and maybe sweet, tricky. I sort of thought they'd be like me. I pictured a blond little girl. Tinkerbell.

They are darker than I imagined. More beautiful. Scarier. Meaner. They are not like me.

Did I think they would be kind, when my mother talked about them?

Yes, maybe I did.

I don't know.

I don't know what I thought. Maybe I never really believed her.

One of the faeries, a strong one—she has tough muscles in her thin arms—comes over to me in the clearing.

"Lucy," she says. "The light one." Her voice is like a broken glass bell.

"Where am I?" I ask, even though I know already.

The faerie looks around. "You've crossed into the faerieground," she says. "You're on Queen Calandra's land now."

The stories are true. I never knew for sure. I suspected, sometimes. Sometimes I didn't. Sometimes it made me mad and annoyed that my mom would believe in faeries, like a little girl. Sometimes it was just embarrassing. Sometimes I thought it was special, something cool and secret that only we really knew about.

I always wondered. Now I know for sure. The stories are true.

"Why am I here?" I ask, even though I know that already too.

She sneers at me. I look down at my body. My clothes are dirty. Leaves linger in my hair. For the first time, I feel afraid.

"You're here because your friend wished you away," she tells me. Then she laughs. "I'm sure you remember that happening."

Of course I do.

I try to stand, but my hands are laced to the ground by braids of grass. "How can I leave?" I ask. "Does she just need to wish me back home?"

Soli, I think. *Wish me home. Please.*

The dark faerie shakes her head. "You're not the one the queen wants," she says. "She wants the dark one. The scared one. The lonely one. The other one."

"Soli?" I ask.

"Yes," the faerie says. "The queen needs Soledad to do something. A . . . favor. When she's done it, you'll be free."

"Can't I do it?" I ask.

"No," she says. "You can't. Soledad has to do it."

"But then that's all?" I ask. "Just a favor?"

The faerie doesn't respond, just gazes down at me.

"What if she doesn't want to do it?" I ask. "This favor for the queen."

The faerie laughs. "Well, forever is a long time," she says.

"How will she know what to do?" I ask.

The faerie laughs again. "We'll send her a message," she tells me.

Soli

Lucy is gone.

I can't sleep. I don't know what happened.

Have the stories come true? The stories about wishing in the woods, about the faeries, all those silly stories her mother's always told?

They can't be true.

There are no faeries. Not in this world.

But the fact remains.

I made a wish.

I wished Lucy away.

At midnight, a rock shatters my window. A leaf is wrapped around it.

I am afraid to touch it.

I am afraid to stand near the broken shards of glass.

There are words scratched into the rock in angry letters.

I can't read them.

The only one I know is *Lucy*.

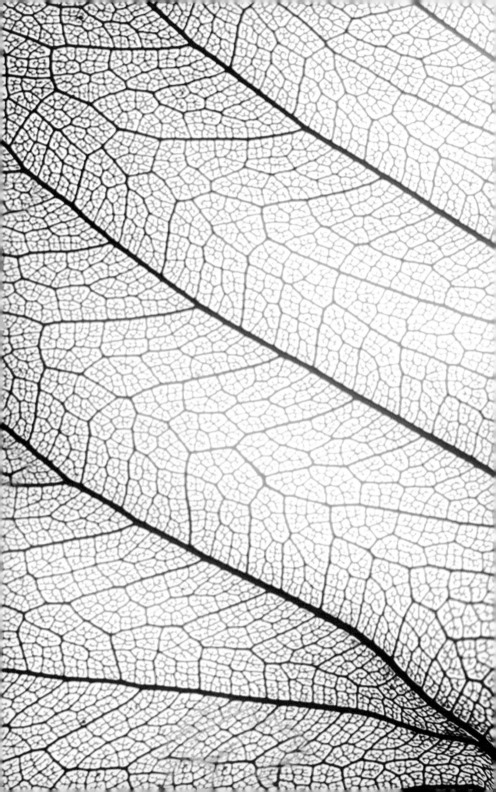

Lucy

My whole life, my mother has left the faeries offerings.

She leaves the gifts at the edge of the woods. Pinned butterflies. Dried lavender. Mushrooms. Rosemary. A small jar of honey. Every time the season changes, she brings them something.

I never go along with her when she leaves these presents. She goes alone, before dawn. The only reason I know is because once I followed her.

Once, I asked her why.

"I angered the queen," she whispered.

It was dark and we sat in lawn chairs in our backyard. Here and there, a firefly sparked.

She reached up to her neck and tangled her fingers in her necklace. She wouldn't tell me anything more. I didn't dare ask.

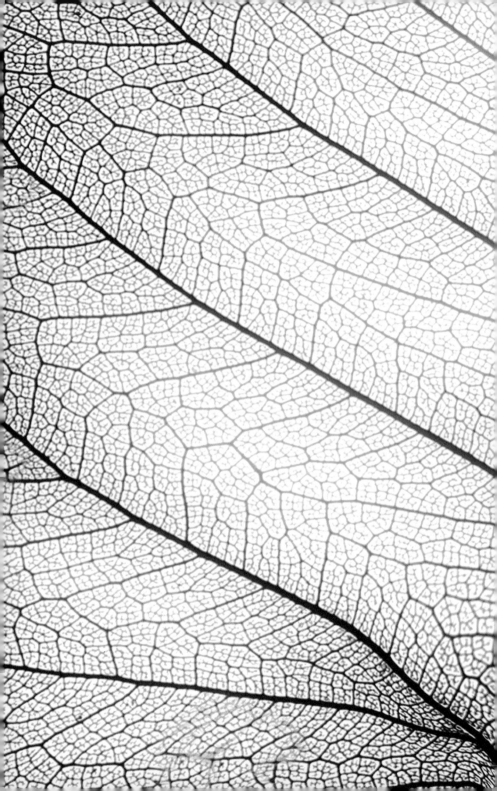

Soli

There's a rock in my hand when I wake up. Yesterday comes rushing back. The wish. The light. Lucy disappearing.

Did it happen?

I stare at the rock.

Yes.

It happened.

Lucy kissed Jaleel, and because of that, I made a wish that she'd disappear.

And because of that, she did.

I get ready for school.
I try to forget that Lucy disappeared.
I try to forget it's my fault.
I try to forget about the wish I made in the woods.

Still, I put the rock in my pocket.

What do I do now? Who would believe me?

I can't go to school.
I can't keep quiet, or pretend to be normal. I can't pretend I didn't wish my friend away. So instead of going to school, I go to Lucy's house.

The rock is a weight in my pocket while I run there, traveling a path I've traveled a thousand times.

Ten thousand, maybe. More.

I don't take the shortcut through the woods. I never liked to take it alone. And right now, I'm afraid of the woods. I don't ever want to go back there.

I never dreamed the stories could be true.

At Lucy's house, I stand on the step. What can I tell Andria? What will she already know?

Will she be worried?
Will she blame me?

I would.

I do, I do blame myself.

Before I can even knock, the front door opens wide. I hold my breath.

Lucy's mom looks at me the way a mother would look at a daughter. She's not my mother, but she might as well be.

She has always taken care of me.

"Hello, Soli," she says. "I've been waiting for you."

Lucy

I'm a prisoner. The faeries want me for something, but I don't know what. It's too dark to see anything where I am, here, in the shadows. My prison is dark and smells like death. I touch the walls in the dark and feel only wet stone. Gross. There's no way out.

Then my hand falls on a body. "Watch it," a voice says. The body moves away.

"Who's there?" I whisper.

"Keep quiet," the boy says. "Don't remind them you're here."

I move back to my corner. "Who are you?" I ask. I try to keep my voice from shaking, but it isn't easy. I'm afraid, and my voice betrays me.

From the other side of the cell, the voice whispers, "My name is Kheelan. Don't be scared. I'm a prisoner too."

"I'm Lucy," I say.

"I know who you are," he says. "The light girl."

What? Light?

My hair, maybe. But how does he know who I am? Who's told him about me?

"What do they want from me?" I ask.

"Queen Calandra wants the dark one. Your friend," Kheelan says. "The one in the shadows."

I forget to whisper. Instead, I laugh. "Soli?" I ask. "Dark?"

Soli isn't dark.

Soli isn't dark at all.

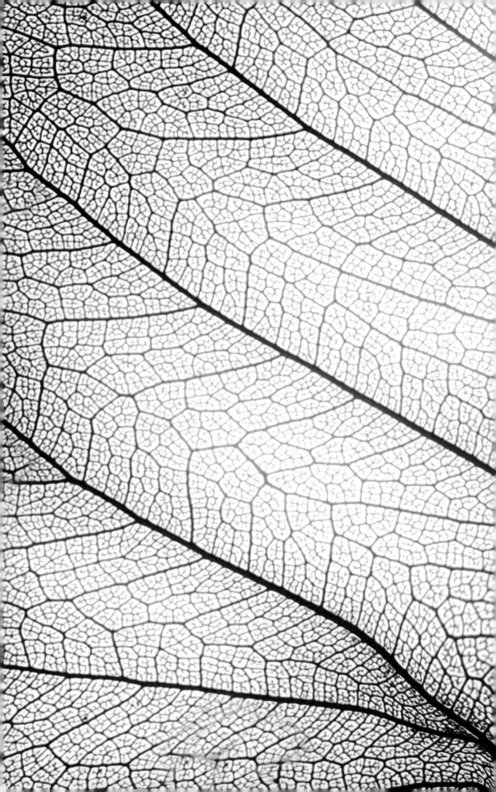

Lucy

When we were five, we promised we'd be best friends forever.

To make the promise, we pretended we were having a faerie ceremony, even though Soli didn't believe in them. Because I wouldn't let her.

Instead, I made it a game. We carved our names in the shadows of an old willow tree. The tree still stands in Willow Forest.

Once, when we were small, Soli found a wounded bird by our tree house. She took it in. She fed the bird and kept it warm. She made a little bed for it in a box, with a pillow made of a rolled-up pair of socks and an old soft rag for a blanket.

She named the bird Henrietta.

As she cared for it, Soli sang to the bird, some sweet old lullaby her mother must have sung to her.

Everything will heal.
Everyone will feel
Better, in the morning.
Better, in the morning.

Soli fed the bird, and dripped water into its open beak. Slowly, it healed. Soon, the bird flew away.

Soli gave that bird its life back.

She gave me my life back too, when my dad died. I couldn't talk about it, afterward. Not to my mom, not to Soli, not to anyone.

After the funeral, Soli came to my house.

"You don't have to talk," she told me. "But we need to be together. And soon you'll feel better. I promise."

We stayed in my room, and she hummed, and she stroked my hair.

Better, in the morning.

She was right. We need to be together. Best friends forever. And look at us now. Fighting over a boy, a boy I barely even cared about.

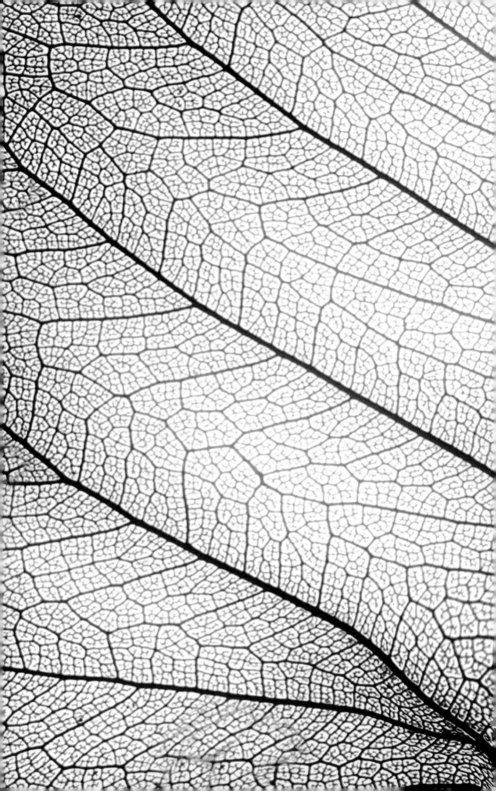

Lucy

"*Why are you here?*" I ask the boy in the other corner of the cell.

"It's a long story. But Queen Calandra thinks I'm rebellious," Kheelan says. I can hear the smile in his voice. "So she's punishing me."

"I guess that makes two of us," I mutter.

"Will your friend come for you?" he asks.

"She's my best friend," I say. I think of our names carved on the old tree. "She'll never leave me here."

"That's part of her plan," he says. "The queen's, I mean. Not your friend's."

"Who is she, anyway?" I ask.

"Calandra?" Kheelan says. "Ah, she's just the queen. She's been around for a while. She is many long stories, not all of them true." He pauses and adds, "Most of them with unhappy endings."

"Is she dangerous?" I ask.

Kheelan laughs. "Dangerous," he repeats. "Is Calandra dangerous."

"I don't know anything about her," I say.

"I know," he whispers. "I'm sorry."

We are quiet for a minute. Then his voice floats across the cell.

"Of course she's dangerous," he says. "But like anything else, she only has power if you let her have it."

"I'm afraid," I whisper.

I feel Kheelan's fingers grasping mine. "Don't be," he says.

A heavy door opens. We move apart. Light creeps in, blinding me.

"The queen will see you now," a deep voice says. Hands grab my shoulders. "Get up," the man says.

I stand up and Kheelan quickly reaches up and grabs my hand.

"Don't let her break you," he whispers. "Be strong, Lucy." He squeezes my fingers, and then lets go.

The guard drags me out from the dark.

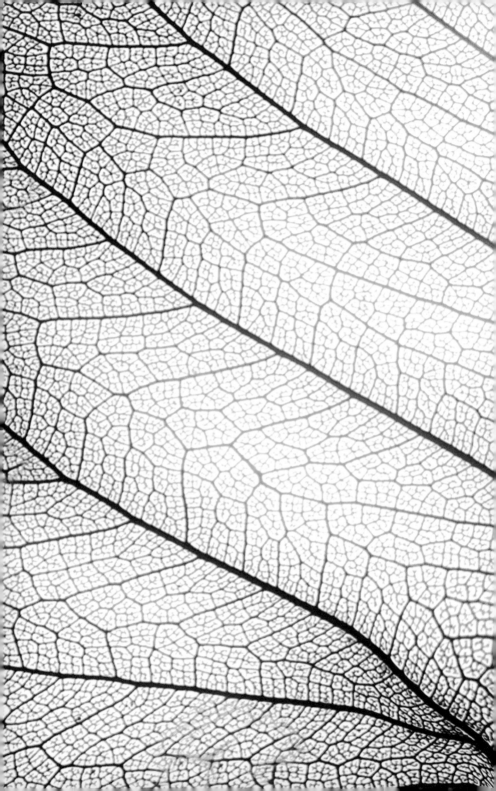

11

Soli

Lucy's mother looks terrible.

"Hi, Andria," I say.

"Do you know where she is?" Lucy's mom asks.

She's worried.

Of course she is.

I forget sometimes that I'm not Lucy's whole world.

I look around. "Can I come in?" I ask.

"Of course," Andria says. "I'm sorry. Yes. Please come in."

I sit down on the couch. Lucy and I have sat here so many times. Will we ever sit together again?

"So?" Andria asks. "Where is she? I'm so worried about her."

"I don't know," I say.

Andria's face turns pale. "When is the last time you saw her?" she asks.

Can I tell her the truth?

That in the forest, I wished her daughter away, and it worked?

That I think faeries took her?

That they sent me a message?

Lucy always pretended not to believe in faeries, but I know Lucy's mom does.

"Lucy is gone because I wished her away," I blurt out.

"What?" Andria whispers. Her eyes grow wide.

"We were in the forest," I say. "Yesterday, after school. I was mad, and . . . " Tears sting my eyes. "I'm sorry," I whisper.

Lucy's mom closes the window. Then she pulls the blinds. Then she locks the door.

"Listen to me very carefully," she says. "Did they try contacting you?"

I pull the rock out of my pocket. Andria's face is white. "This came through my window," I tell her. "Lucy's name is on it." I hold it out to her.

Andria grabs the rock.

She turns it over in her hands.

She rubs her thumb across Lucy's name.

"Do you know what it says?" I ask.

Andria reads the strange letters. "A faerie's contract has been made. Come to Willow's Gate to find Lucy."

She swallows hard. "It's the faerie language," she tells me.

"I can't believe they're real," I say.

"Oh, they're real," Andria says.

Something in her voice tells me to not question her.

"How do we get her back?" I ask.

Andria sighs. "We don't, Soli," she says. "You do. You're the only way."

"How?" I whisper.

"You have to go to them," she tells me. "No one else can do this."

"What do I do?" I ask, trying to be brave.

"Go to the depths of Willow Forest alone," she tells me. "Find a four-leaf clover. Then pull each of its leaves. When they're gone, say your wish."

"No way," I say. "I'm never wishing in the forest again."

"You need to wish to see a faerie. Otherwise the door will be invisible to you," Andria explains. "And if the door stays invisible, we'll never get Lucy back."

"Okay," I whisper.

Whatever it takes.

A hunt for a four-leaf clover in the middle of the woods.

Andria gazes at me. Then she takes off her necklace. A silver shape hangs from a thin silver strand.

"Take this," she says. "It will protect you."

"It's beautiful," I say, gazing at the delicate necklace. "Where did you get it? How do you know it will keep me safe?"

Andria's face turns dark. "An old friend gave it to me for doing her a favor," she says. "Don't tell any of the faeries about it. It might be worth something to them. You might

be able to trade it. I'm not sure what it means to them. My friend never told me. But save it for a last resort and don't give it to the queen." She stands up. "Now. Go."

I look down at the charm on the chain. It's a four-leaf clover trapped inside a three-ring circle.

Then I secure the chain around my neck. The charm drops down to my heart, and I tuck it inside my shirt.

"What should I do once I'm there?" I ask. "In the faerieground, I mean. How do I get Lucy back?"

"Find the queen's secret," she says. "The wish that keeps her captive there. But be careful. She's crafty. She'll trick you."

I stand to leave, but Andria stops me. "Wait a minute. I almost forgot. There's something else you might need," she says.

She rummages in a closet and pulls out a jar.

Just a simple old glass jar.

"What is this for?" I ask.

Andria shrugs. "It's always good to have a jar. You'll see."

I put the jar in my knapsack.

"Bring her back," Andria whispers.

The next thing I know, I'm running toward Willow Forest.

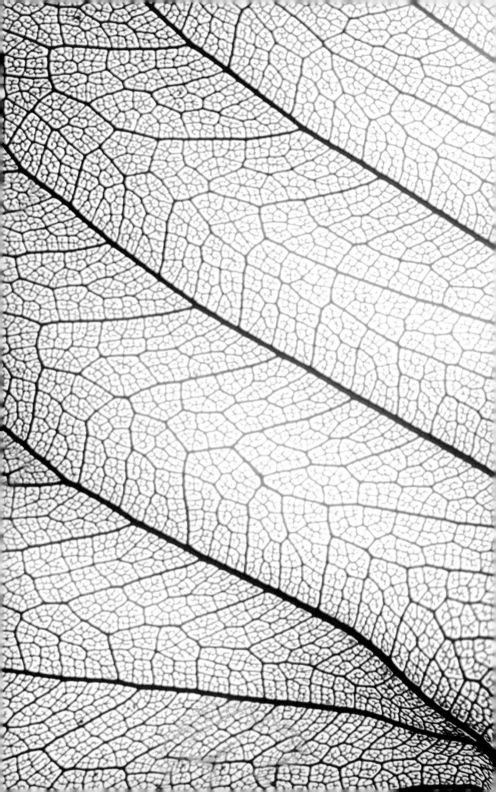

Soli

Once we were in the woods, Lucy and I, playing a game.

I don't remember what the game was, only that I was hiding, and Lucy was supposed to find me.

It grew dark. Cold. I kept waiting.

The woods, once a playground, became scary.
I waited and waited and waited.

I knew my way out of the woods. I knew the woods like I knew my own face, or my mother's face. I knew exactly where I was and how to get home from there.

So as the woods became darker and darker and colder and colder, I could have stood up, brushed the dirt off my clothes, and walked home. I would not have been afraid.

That's not what I did.

I believed Lucy would find me.

And she did.

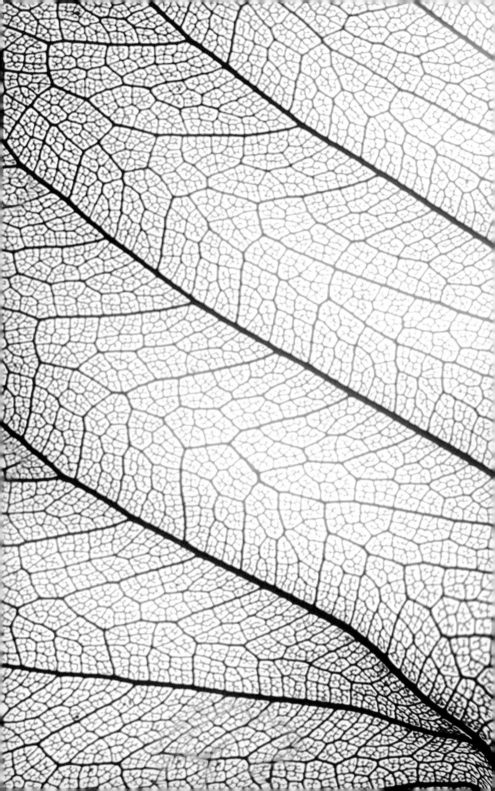

Lucy

When you think of faeries, you think of light.

Sweetness. Joy.

Queen Calandra's palace has none of those things. It's cold and damp and dark. Spiderwebs cling to the walls.

The guard brings me to a stone-walled room. Candles burn on a table. And of course there is a throne.

"She is here," the guard says. He pushes me forward. Then the doors slam behind me.

"Do you have it?" a woman's voice asks, rising from the near shadows.

"Have what?" I ask. I look down at myself. I have nothing except my clothes.

"The necklace. Your mother's necklace," the queen says. Then I see her. Queen Calandra. She is beautiful and dangerous. She doesn't look like the other faeries. She is more solid, and also more terrifying.

"The necklace!" the queen snaps. Her voice is a whip bent across the room.

"No, I don't have it," I say. "She never takes it off."

It's the truth. My mother has worn that necklace forever. As long as I can remember, anyway.

"Then you'll have to wait until someone brings it," the queen says. "You may as well make yourself at home in the prison."

"This isn't my home," I say. "Please, just let me go. I can make sure you get what you want."

"No," the queen says. "I don't trust humans."

Then her eyes glow. "Unless you make a wish, that is."

"What kind of wish?" I ask.

"Wish for that friend of yours to take your place," she says. "Trade places with your friend. Send her here, free yourself."

"I could never do that to Soli," I whisper. "If that is my only way out, there is no way out." I won't betray Soli, not again, not ever.

"Imagine being back home, the comfort," the queen says. Her voice drips with sweetness.

"Stop it," I say. "Stop."

"Your own bed. How soft it would be, after a night spent on stone! How warm, how welcome! Wouldn't you love to sleep in your own room again, your mother in the next room, protecting you?" the queen whispers, a sugar-spun smile crossing her face like a flicker.

"Stop," I moan.

"The gentle arms of your mother, embracing you," she says. "Your mother! All you have to do is wish her here, your friend. Soledad. And then you can be with your mother again. A simple trade. An easy bargain."

"I won't do it," I say. I make my voice as strong as I can. Strong like my mother. "I won't do that to Soli."

"She wished you away!" the queen says. The honey is gone from her voice.

"I'm not her," I say.

The queen laughs. "No," she says. "No, you're not. But you're close."

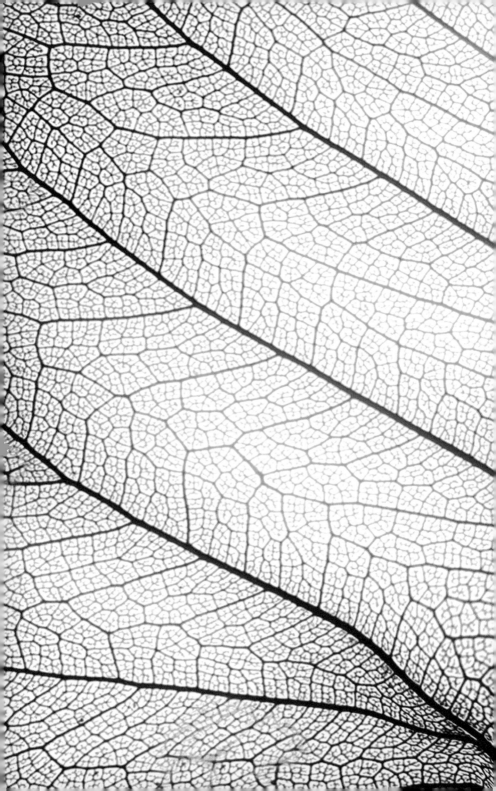

Soli

In the forest, I stop running. I find the place where Lucy and I were yesterday.

The undergrowth is matted where we sat, where we fought.

I know wishes are heard here.

I reach up and touch the charm around my neck. Find a four-leaf clover? This could take hours.

But. I have to do it.

I drop to my knees. It's dark in the forest, even though it's still morning.

As I pick through the clover, one firefly blinks nearby. Soon, it's joined by another, then another. They cluster over a patch of clover in the shadows beneath a thick, old tree.

I set down my backpack and hear the clunk of Andria's jar hitting the ground.

When we were little, Lucy and I loved trapping fireflies in jars. Some kids squashed the bugs and used their guts to paint lit words.

The light only lasted a minute.

Lucy and I didn't want to hurt the fireflies. We just thought they were beautiful.

When we put them in jars, they'd blink at us, like an old-time message. Lucy and I would make up meanings, pretend we knew what the fireflies were saying.

Now, without Lucy, I gaze at the fireflies. There are more now, maybe a dozen. Their lights flash in rhythm over a patch of clover.

I reach out my hand, but none fly to me. They stay where they are.

When I walk over, they swarm away.

I reach down, and the first thing my fingers touch is a four-leaf clover.

A tangle of fireflies is caught in my hair.

And when I open my backpack, Andria's jar is full of fireflies, and the lid is tightly sealed.

I close my eyes, pulling the clover leaves one by one.

"I wish to see faeries," I whisper.

I pour my heart into the wish.

I wish it more than I've ever wished anything.

And then I hear a whisper.

"Follow."

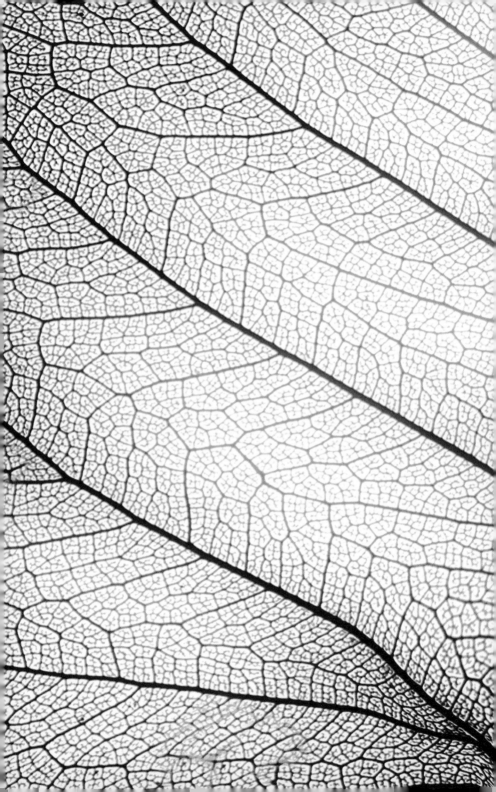

Lucy

The guard throws me back into the cold stone room where Kheelan still waits. In the light from the opened door, I can see him, bound by iron chains to the wall.

After the door slams shut, we are blind again. But only for a moment. There's a tiny window high above Kheelan's head.

I wouldn't even think of escaping—it's only a few inches tall and a few inches wide. But now that the sun is out, enough light streams in to see by.

He has dark hair and eyes. In a way, he reminds me of Soli. The way her gaze feels hot, almost. Like she can see inside me. Kheelan's gaze feels like that.

"You're back," he says. "How was it?"

"I don't know," I say. "I think I made her mad."

He nods. "But you didn't do what she asked," he says.

"No," I say. "No, I didn't."

"That's good," Kheelan says. "With Queen Calandra, it's never just what she says. Never just the one promise. It ends up being a million horrible things, but you already agreed, and you can't take it back."

"You can't take back a wish?" I ask.

"No," Kheelan says. "Never. It's a bond between faeries, a contract."

"Between faeries?" I repeat. "But Soli and I aren't faeries."

Kheelan smiles. His smile looks like Soli's, too.

Soli

The fireflies guide me.

The woods grow darker. Soon, I stand in front of an old willow tree. Years ago, Lucy and I carved our names into that tree's trunk, close to the ground, in the shadows.

I bend and see that our names are still there. My finger traces the letters.

"What do you want?" a voice asks.

I jump up and look around, but no one is there.

"What do you want?" the voice repeats. The tree's branches sprawl in all directions, gating me in.

"Um, I got a message. See?" I say, taking the rock from my pocket.

"They're waiting for you," the voice tells me.

The tree creaks at its roots.
A door opens.

"You may enter, Soli Meddow," the voice whispers.

I'm scared to go in. It's dark and cold in there. I don't know what's inside.

Unknown.

Well, not totally unknown. I know two things.

First, that Lucy is in there.

And second, that we are supposed to be together.

I take a deep breath, close my eyes, and step into the darkness.

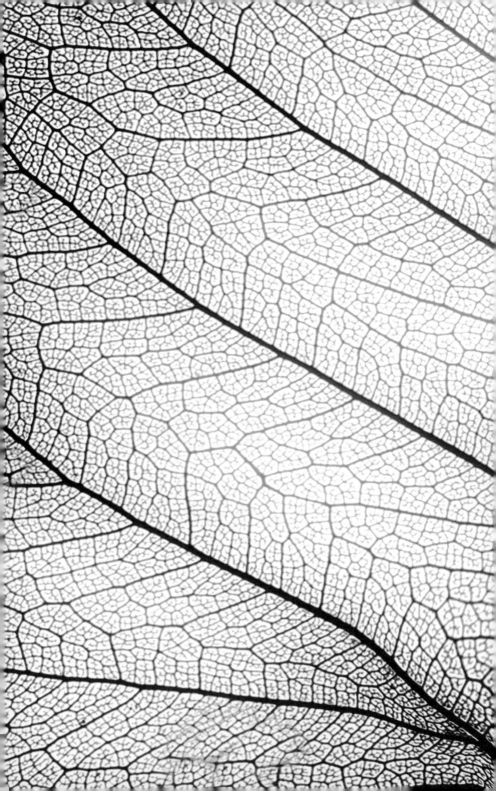

Lucy

I cry myself to sleep on the stone floor of Queen Calandra's prison.

I dream I'm back at school, yelling at Jaleel. He looks scared and shocked. I scream at him, over and over. He tries to run away, but he can't. I try to run away, but I can't. I am made to stand there, yelling, tears falling down my face and collecting in a puddle at my feet.

I dream I'm at home, in my room, in my bed, in my blankets. I can hear my mother's voice. She's talking about me. Saying I'm missing, saying she doesn't know where I am, saying I'm gone. Then she says she doesn't care, and she laughs, and she sounds happy. Free.

I dream I am at my father's funeral.

I'm terrified and sad, and I can't find Soli.

When I ask my mother where she is, my mother says she's never heard of anyone named Soli, who would name a child Soli, what kind of name is that anyway?

When I try to remind her of Soli, my almost-sister, my best friend, my mother just laughs and laughs and laughs.

I dream I'm in the woods, running after Soli.

I know she's angry with me. I chase her and chase her through the woods, ending up at the old willow tree where our names are carved. When she turns around and sees my face, she smiles, and she stretches her hands out. I run to hug her, and just as I'm about to wrap my arms around her, she disappears.

Part 3

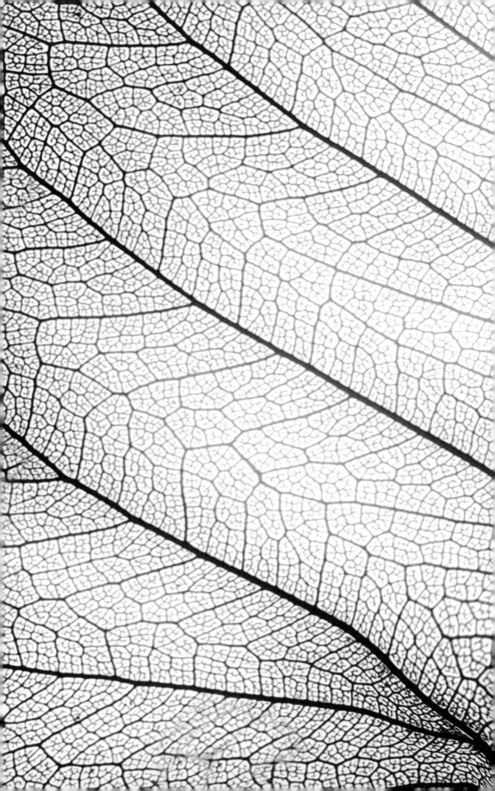

Soli

I'm here.

The faerieground is beautiful and scary.

As soon as I'm here, I wish I wasn't.

My wish isn't the kind of wish that sent Lucy away. That wish was spoken and not true. Or not really true, anyway.

This wish is different.

A true wish. A secret inside wish.

I try to cover it up with bravery.

I try to turn my skeleton to steel, so nothing can hurt me.

I try to be fire, so nothing can stop me.

I try to stand bravely in the forest.

My mother always said I was brave, but I never believed her. After all, I spend so much time hiding, in the shadows. Not being brave.

I don't think of myself like that.

Lately I'm realizing that I don't really know what I think of myself. Besides that I'm Lucy's friend. That's all I really know.

Lucy is the measure I measure myself by.

I think Lucy is brave.

My mother is brave, and my brother even more so. It might run in the family, but I'm adopted. My birth mother could have been brave.

I don't know.

I never knew her.

Maybe she was brave.

I used to be, I guess.

My mother always tells this story about when I was a little girl.

I would walk right up to the road.

I would wait for cars to pass.

And walk across. Just like that.

Also, when I was a little girl, I would introduce myself to strangers. I would smile and put out my hand and say, "I'm Soli. Who are you?"

So maybe there's something brave inside me after all.

Maybe it was the small, brave part of me that wished Lucy away and then also the small, brave part of me that followed her here.

And I know that it is the small, brave part of me that takes the first small step into the faerieground.

When I feel something watching me, and I start to run, is that the brave part of me or the scared part?

Does it matter, if it's all to find Lucy and bring her home?

Lucy

I can't believe I ever complained that my room at home was too small.

Now that I'm spending my second night in a prison cell, that little room at home seems like heaven. This cell smells like mold. It's dark and I'm freezing. I'm miserable. And I'm afraid. How long will my life be like this? How long before the queen gets what she wants and Soli and I can just go back to life the way it was?

I make a promise to myself. Once I'm home, I won't even look at Jaleel, unless it's to tell him about how wonderful Soli is. I'll never kiss him again.

And even as I'm making that promise, promising it to whatever can hear inside my head, I know I don't want to keep it.

I will, if I have to. But I don't want to have to.

I sigh and try to find a comfortable spot on the stone floor, but it's terrible.

Kheelan is sleeping on his side of the cell. He's been here a while. He's used to it. But I can't sleep here.

I hear voices through our tiny little window. Footsteps, walking faster and faster. When the voices get closer, I can hear what they're saying.

"Yes, the dark one," a man's voice says. "She's here."

"Here? But how—" a woman begins.

The thumping of my heart drowns them out as they move farther away.

The dark one. That's what they keep calling Soli.

The dark one is here, the man said.

Soli, here? Has she come to find me?

"Kheelan, are you awake?" I whisper.

I hear his body moving on the floor. "No," he says.

"I need your help," I say. "Soli is here. We have to find her. I don't know if she can protect herself."

"Your friend is here?" he asks. I hear him shift in the darkness. "Are you sure?"

"Yes," I say.

"How do you know?" he asks. "Do you two share some kind of signal, or something?"

I sigh. "No. I heard the guards talking," I tell him. "Can you get me out of here?"

He laughs. "If I could get you out, wouldn't I get myself out first?" he says. But his voice has changed. I can tell he's thinking about it.

"Then get yourself out," I say. "And find my friend. She needs our help. She can't do this on her own. Once you find her, you can come back for me."

I don't trust Kheelan. Not completely. He could be a murderer. He could be insane. After all, he's in prison, and all I know is that he angered the queen. I don't know what he did to make her angry.

And he doesn't trust me. Not completely. And why should he? What does he know about me? That I'm a human who suddenly found herself in enemy territory. I could be a spy, I could be someone come to hurt them all.

We don't trust each other.

But we're all we have.

"Please," I whisper.

"Fine," he says. "I have to come up with a plan."

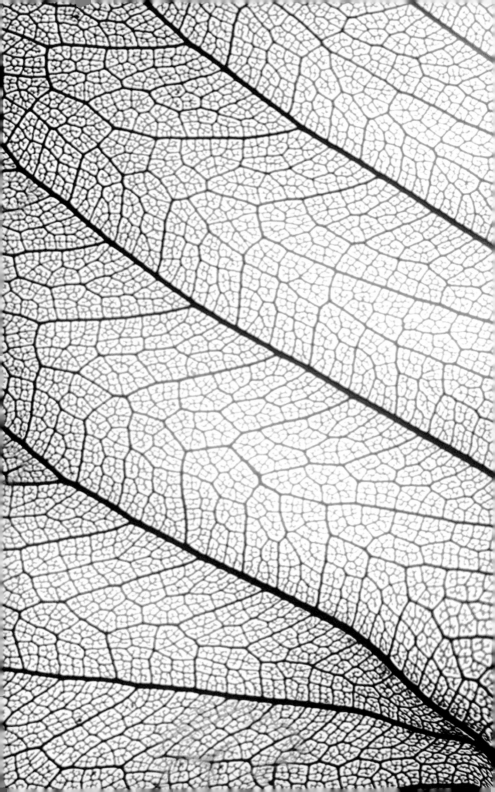

18

Lucy

It seems like hours pass in the cold, cobwebby silence of our cell.

I even fall asleep. It could have been for five minutes, or it could have been a day.

Then, suddenly, Kheelan screams. "Guards!" he yells. "The girl, the human! She's escaping! Hurry!"

"What are you doing?" I whisper.

Kheelan is crouched next to me, an animal waiting to pounce. A cat who's found a mouse.

"Play along," he says. He yells again, "Guards! Hurry!"

We hear voices, shouts, a whistle blowing. Heavy footsteps pound up to our cell's door. Iron keys slip into the locks.

I hold my breath. The door opens, and Kheelan launches himself at the guards, pushes past them, is gone.

Soli

The thing chases me through the forest. Its footsteps pound behind me. Until I find myself running into a cast-iron gate.

Then the thing is gone.
The forest is quiet.

Whatever it was, it led me here. Maybe it was chasing me. Maybe it was herding me to this place.

My clothes and shoes are soaked and muddy from my run. I wipe sweat from my face and look around.

Beyond the gate is a bright green garden. The wildflowers are familiar but not quite right, like flowers in a dream.

And beyond the garden is a river, and beyond the river is the castle.

And Lucy must be inside that castle.

So that is where I need to go.

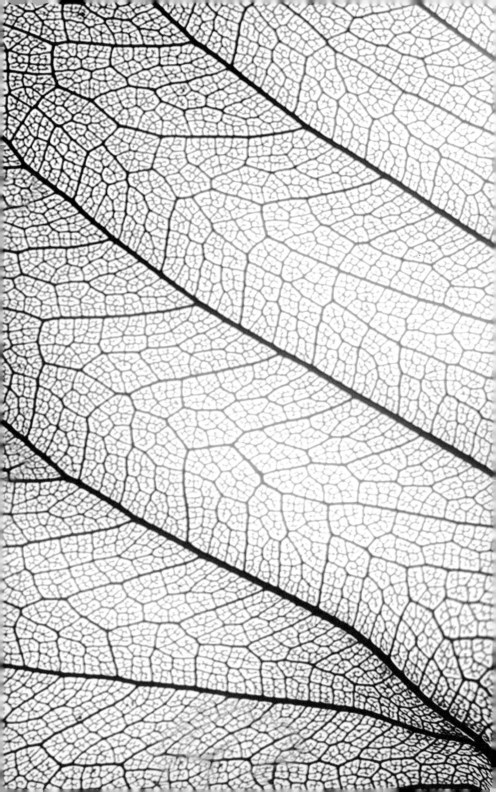

Lucy

After Kheelan escapes, the guards take me to Queen Calandra. They aren't gentle at all. They're mad at me. They think I helped him. They think it's my fault. I don't deny it. I don't say anything.

Last time, they took me to talk to the queen in the throne room. This time they take me somewhere else. They drag me deeper and deeper within the palace.

It's not a palace like I always imagined, beautiful and golden. It's more like a dungeon, all of it, or a nightmare.

The floors are dirty. Spiders—and worse—nest on the walls. The few lit candles are bent or broken.

It seems like it used to be beautiful.

It seems like something really bad must have happened here.

Before I can look much more, the guards push me inside a room and slam the doors behind me.

This must be where she lives. There's a fireplace, a squat velvet sofa next to a lantern, some bookshelves. It's comfortable-looking, homelike. Fresh-cut flowers sit in a pretty vase upon the mantle.

There's a painting of the queen over the fireplace. She's holding something. A baby?

In the room, a tall figure stands in the soft light. It's Queen Calandra, of course, and I can already tell she is angry.

The queen's eyes look even blacker in the shadows against her fair skin. Her thin wings hover over her shoulders. Her crown, made out of twigs, makes her look painful, and also in pain.

The guards have left me alone with her. I am afraid,

but I know I need to be brave. So I decide to play dumb. Gain her trust. What choice do I have?

"Where is Kheelan?" she asks me.

"That crazy guy who escaped?" I say. I shrug. "I have no idea. Last time I checked, crazy people don't, like, tell you where they're going when they escape from prison."

"My guards say you didn't try to run," she says. "Did he tell you he was leaving? Why didn't you go?"

"He told me he made you mad," I say, meeting her eyes. That's true, at least. "That's the last thing I want to do. Why would I try to escape with him?"

Queen Calandra sits down on the sofa. My eyes drift to its soft cushions. After more than a day in a stone cell, all I want is a comfortable place to sit. As if she can read my mind, the queen says, "Come. Sit."

I hesitate only for a moment before doing what she says.

This is the closest I've been to her. She leans close to me, brushes hair out of my face, smiles sweetly. Then she whispers, "There is punishment in my kingdom for liars."

I feel my blood turn cold.

She goes on, "If I find out that lies came from your pretty mouth, you will suffer times three. Understand?"

I swallow hard and nod. "Yes," I say. "I understand."

She gets up and paces silently. I look up at the painting above the fireplace. It's the queen sitting on this same velvet sofa. She is holding a baby. A dark-haired, dark-eyed little girl. The baby is wearing a necklace. I recognize it—it's just like my mother's pendant.

And the baby's eyes remind me so much of Soli.

Soli

No matter how far I walk, the castle doesn't seem to get any closer.

It just gets more frightening.

The building, even from this distance, is dark, dirty, crumbling. Not what I ever would have imagined a faerie castle to be.

Not that I ever spent much time imagining faerie castles.

The necklace around my throat feels warm, like it could burn me. Still, I tuck it into my shirt. Its warmth bounces against me as I run.

Just as I'm ready to give up, I hear footsteps behind me.

I close my eyes and stand still. I don't have the energy to try to outrun anyone now. I hold on to Andria's necklace.

Then I hear my name. A whisper. "Soli."

I stop breathing.

I drop my necklace back into my sweater. It dangles near my heart.

When I turn, a boy is standing there. He smiles.

"Hello," he says. "Don't run."

I want to run, of course. But—for some reason, I'm not afraid.

The boy has beautiful, sharp features and dark, dark hair. It shines under the moonlight.

When he takes another step closer, I see his green eyes.

And after another step, I see his wings.

"Your friend sent me," he says. "Lucy." He smiles. "I can see you're still afraid," he adds. "But you don't need to be. I'm here to help you."

"Who are you?" I ask, my voice hoarse.

He smiles again. "Kheelan," he says. "My name is Kheelan. And I'm on your side in this fight."

This fight.

At first I think for some reason he means the fight between me and Lucy over Jaleel from school. The fight that made me make the wish that sent her here.

But that isn't the fight he means, of course.

"There are many of us on your side," Kheelan goes on.

"Who—who are you fighting against?" I ask.

He frowns. "There's so much you need to learn," he tells me. "We don't have time right now. You need to get to the queen."

"Yes," another voice says. "The queen is waiting."

I gasp and turn.

Guards surround us in a matter of seconds. Kheelan looks like a wild animal, not ready to be caged in.

This isn't part of his plan.

"We are the ones they fight against," one of them says, stepping forward.

"And we're here to bring you to the queen," says another. "She's been waiting for you."

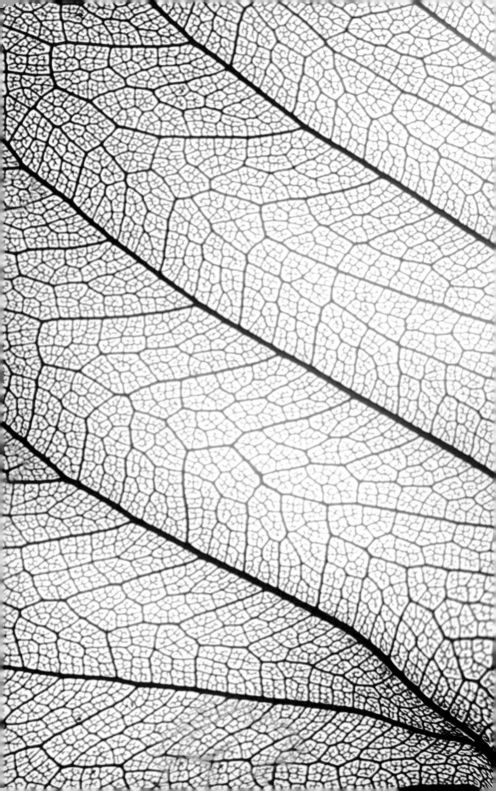

Lucy

She sends me back to my cell, empty now without Kheelan there.

I sink down, put my head on my knees, and cry. Then, thank goodness, I fall asleep. I don't know how much time has passed when I wake up, but light is streaming through the cell's small window.

Just after I wake up, two guards come in to get me. This time they are gentler.

"Where are you bringing me?" I ask as we walk down the hall. I don't want to go back to her room. I'd rather be in the throne room than in her private space. For some reason, she's more frightening there.

"The throne room," one of the guards says. Her companion shoots him a look, but the first guard just shrugs.

When they throw the doors open to the throne room, the first thing I see is the queen. She looks angrier than ever.

"The next ten minutes will test you, light one," she tells me. Her voice is almost a growl. She gestures to the guards and says, "Put the girl into the silence box."

The guards grab my arms and drag me to a glass box.

"You'll be able to see, but unseen," the queen says. Then she slams the door closed.

Through the box, I watch as more guards walk in. One is holding Kheelan's arms, struggling. Soli walks right behind him. Her chin is up. Still, she looks scared.

I pound on the glass. "Soli!" I scream, loud—my voice makes my ears ring. "Soli!"

She can't hear me. She doesn't look at me.

The queen laughs. I'm a spectator to my friend's fate.

This is my test.

"Welcome," the queen says to Soli. "Kheelan, welcome back."

The guards force Kheelan to his knees in front of the Queen. Soli's eyes go wide, watching his struggle.

I can't stop feeling happy to see her. My best friend looks tired, like she hasn't slept in days. Her clothes are covered in mud. Her backpack is slung over her shoulder, just like after a school day.

"I know why you're here," the queen says.

"To get my friend back," Soli says. Her voice shakes, but it's clear.

The queen laughs. "Undo a wish made on faerieground?" she says, shaking her head. "That won't happen."

Soli's hands go to her throat. "I didn't mean to," she whispers. "It was a mistake. I was angry."

The queen laughs again, a bitter, angry chuckle. "A mistake?" she says. "I know mistakes."

She glares at the guards and Kheelan. "Leave us," she says.

"No!" Kheelan yells, struggling to his feet.

But the guards pull him out and slam the door. I can hear his cries coming from the hall.

And without him in the room, I am suddenly more afraid than ever.

Soli

We are alone now, the queen and I.

She returns her gaze to me. "So you want your friend back," the queen says. "What would you do to get her back?"

I try to steady my voice, to make myself seem more sure.

"I'd—I'd do anything, I guess," I say. "Like I said, it was a terrible mistake. I'm sure you'd understand."

The queen glances at a tall glass box in the corner. "Would you promise to never see your friend again?" she asks.

I frown, thinking.

Never speak to Lucy again?
Never see her?
Never laugh with her?

Then I stand up straight. "If it meant she was safe, yes. I'd do anything."

She raises one dark eyebrow. "Then I have just the job," she says. "I'm going to send you to get something for me. Something that belongs to me. Something that was taken from me."

She opens her mouth like she has more to say, but she stops.

"What is it?" I ask.

"The Dark Crown," she says. "It's hidden underneath the Black Lake. Only a human can retrieve it, but it is mine."

She's lying, but I don't know what she's lying about. I assume it's about who owns the crown. I don't care.

If getting this crown will make Lucy safe, I'll do it.

"If I get it, can I see Lucy again?" I ask. "Can we go home?"

"You have my word," the queen says.

I don't know why, but I believe her.

"I need a guide," I say. "I don't know this place at all. Someone has to help me."

"Two birds, one stone," the queen murmurs.

Then, louder, she says, "I'll send the boy with you. Kheelan. And if he escapes, you'll suffer his punishment instead. You have two sundowns."

"I want to see Lucy before I leave," I whisper.

The queen laughs. "Get out," she says.

Lucy

Soon I am back in my cell.

I don't know where the queen sent Soli, but I'm starting to think both of us will die here.

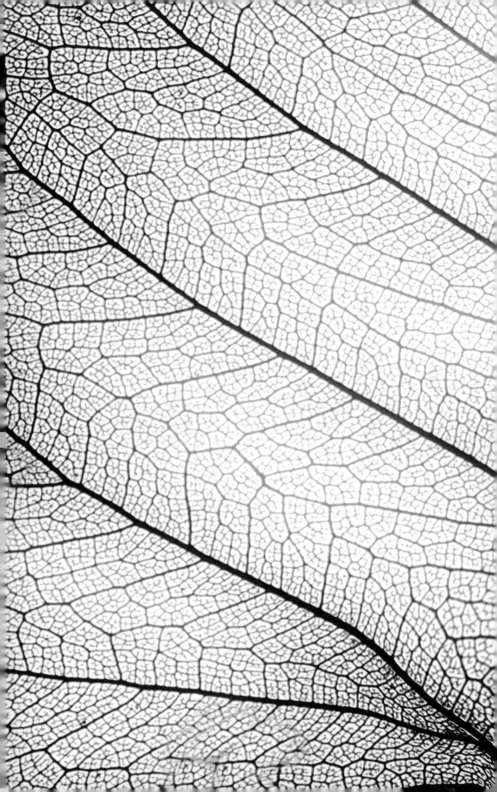

Soli

Kheelan and I walk for miles.

He knows his turf. He climbs rocks and trees like nothing I've ever seen before.

I struggle to keep up with him.

I keep worrying that he's going to run off into the woods and leave me alone.

After all, what reason could he have to help me?

But he doesn't leave me behind. He helps me every step of the way.

The forest is my forest, only it's not.
I know it but I don't know it.

I keep thinking I recognize things—a stream, a pile of rocks, a particular tree—but then when I look closer, it's not the same at all.

Still, I can tell I'm in Willow Forest. But I know I'm nowhere near home.

The sky is lightening with sunrise when he stops and grabs my hand. "Right over there, do you see the smoke?" he asks, pointing. Red smoke curls on the horizon.

"Yes," I say. I brush sweaty hair out of my face. "What is it?"

"That's where the Ladybirds live," Kheelan tells me.

As we get closer, the smoke fills the sky. "Do you know them?"

"No," I say. "Who are they?"

He pauses, then says, "They're our wise ones."

"Like the elders or something?" I ask.

He laughs. "You could say that," he says. "Some of them are five centuries old."

I gasp. "Are they—are they faeries, like you?"

But before he can answer, a loud voice says, "This is Ladybird land. Who are you?" A woman wearing red steps out from behind a tree. She's aiming a bow and arrow at us.

"I am Kheelan, of Roseland," Kheelan says. "And this is Soledad—"

"I know who she is," the woman says.

And she bends down, as if she's bowing.

When she straightens up again, she doesn't meet my eyes.

"We are going to the Black Lake," I say, trying to be brave. "The queen asked me to—"

"The queen?" the Ladybird says. "She can't have the Dark Crown, if that's what she wants."

Nervous, I reach for the necklace around my throat. When I pull out the pendant and rub it between my fingers, Kheelan takes a step back.

"Where—where did you get that?" he asks.

I look down and drop it back beneath my sweater. "Home," I say. "It's Lucy's mom's. She sent it with me when I came to find Lucy. I don't really get why, but—"

The Ladybird smiles and interrupts me. "I'm sure she knew what she was doing," she says.

Then she gestures toward the smoke. "Come. Follow me."

She stalks off through the woods, and we follow behind her.

Kheelan says, "That was—"

"Surprising?" I say, cutting him off.

"To say the least," he says. "Soli, the Ladybirds are seer faeries. That's part of why they stay secluded."

"Creepy," I say, watching the woman ahead of us. "I wouldn't want that. To know so much, about everyone."

"Nobody does," he says.

The Ladybird leads us to a camp made up of tents built from twigs and leaves. The red smoke is coming from the center tent.

There are no men faeries here, so right away, I feel Kheelan's discomfort.

But they don't notice him.

They all stare at me.

"Motherbird will see you now," the woman who led me here says. She nods at the tent. "Your friend must stay outside."

The tent is full of smoke, but I see a figure inside. "Come in," a rich, deep voice says. An old, wrinkly hand reaches out from the smoke. "You are here for the Dark Crown," she says.

It isn't a question.

"Sort of," I say. "I'm here to save my friend."
"The Dark Crown will save your friend?" Motherbird asks. "Tell me how."

I take a deep breath and tell her the whole story.

Even the embarrassing part, the part where the boy I like kissed my best friend and I, angry and jealous and hurt, wished her away.

Then how I traveled here, how the fireflies showed me the way.

Then the chase through the woods, and Kheelan in the palace grounds.

The queen, with her frightening eyes and the human-sized glass box.

Even the necklace, which now burns against my skin. I pull it out and show it to her.

"Can you help me?" I ask.

The woman cocks her head and looks at me. "I can bring you to the Black Lake, and I can help you get the Dark Crown," she says. "But you must never let it touch that woman's hands."

"The queen?" I ask. "But she said it was hers."

"It isn't," Motherbird says. "It is yours."

Lucy

They bring me to her rooms again.

She is angry. I can feel her anger before they even open the door. I hear a bottle break against the stone floor. One of the guards knocks, but she screams, "Wait!"

Someone is in there with her. Someone with a low voice. I can't hear what the low-voiced someone says. I can only hear the queen. "The Ladybirds found her first," she is saying. "That's what you're telling me. That the Ladybirds found her. Again."

The voice says something in a soft, reassuring tone.

But the queen just laughs, a wild, crazy, angry laugh.

"That's ridiculous," she says. "Of course they know who she is. Even if she doesn't have the necklace, any idiot can see she's my daughter. And the Ladybirds know everything. Those old witches know. They know because they're the ones who took her from me."

The guard knocks again. "Should we bring her back to the dungeon?" he asks through the door.

The queen throws the door open. "No," she says. "Bring her in." And when she stares at me this time, all I can see are Soli's eyes.

Part 4

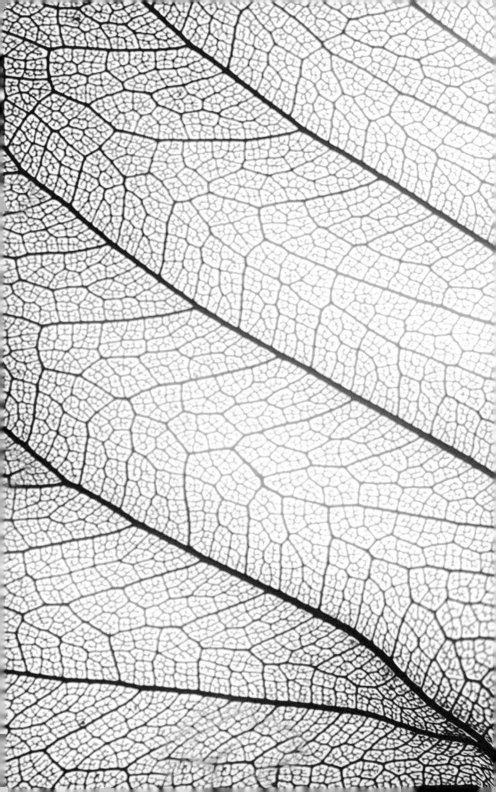

Lucy

The queen shoots angry looks at me as the guard pushes me into her chambers.

I don't know what's going on.

Since Soli left with Kheelan, I've been locked in my cell. I can't imagine why Queen Calandra would want to bring me back here to her rooms.

The queen slams the door in the guard's face. Then she pushes me down onto the sofa.

Her eyes—the queen's, Soli's eyes—are angry.

"You are Andria's daughter," she says. It isn't a question.

"Yes," I say, sitting up straight. I am proud of my mother.

Queen Calandra's nostrils flare. "Your mother is a witch," she says. The way she spits out the word makes me afraid to laugh.

Instead, I picture my mother.

My mother, a witch?

My mother, the calm, sweet, loving woman I know. A nurse, a healer. My mother—who has left offerings for the faeries as long as I can remember, sweet little gifts, sprigs of lavender, willowbuds, cattails, butterfly wings—a witch?

But I do know that she angered the queen, and I do know she'd never tell me why.

"She isn't a witch," I say, as bravely as I can. "She's a nurse."

Queen Calandra laughs. "Right," she says. "A nurse."

"She is!" I say. "She helps deliver babies and she takes care of sick kids."

The queen's face grows dark. Her eyes narrow. "I bet she takes care of kids," she says. "After all, she stole mine."

I can't help it. I glance up at the oil painting above the sofa.

The baby nestled in the queen's arms, like a blossom in its bud.

"Is—is that your baby?" I ask.

"Yes," the queen says. Then she laughs, an angry little laugh. "Or she was, anyway. Until your mother took her."

Then she tells me the story.

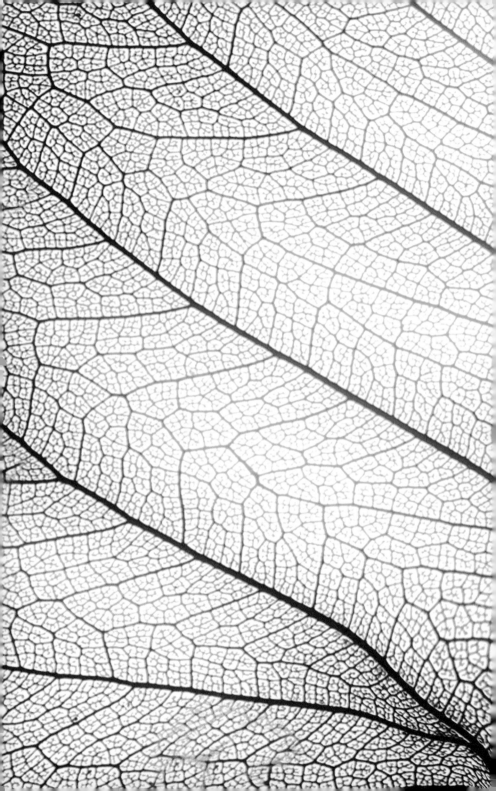

Soli

Night is falling again.

Kheelan and I follow Motherbird through the forest toward Black Lake.

I know this isn't my forest, really, but I can't shake the feeling that I know it.

Like a place I visited in a dream.

"This way," Motherbird says, lifting a branch so that we can pass underneath it.

It's the first time she's spoken to me since we were in her tent. When she told me the Dark Crown belonged to me.

I tried to get her to explain, but she wouldn't.

I can't decide if she's crazy.
Maybe everyone here is.
Maybe I am.

Only I know I'm not.

As we walk, I finally have time to ask Kheelan some of the things I've been wondering about.
Like: why didn't the queen just get the Dark Crown for herself?
Why do I have to go and get it?

"She can't," he says. "They put a spell on it and buried it deep." He glances at me and adds, "And it's not hers, anyway."

I shudder. I haven't told him what Motherbird said, that the crown is mine.

He'll think I'm crazy, or that she is.

"Whose is it?" I ask, trying to act casual.

"You don't know any of our history?" he asks.

Around us, the woods grow more open. I hear water, the rushing of a nearby river.

We must be getting close.

"No," I say. "How would I? I mean, until yesterday—" I pause, trying to count the days since I wished Lucy away—"or the day before, I guess, I didn't even believe in faeries."

"Really?" Kheelan says, smiling. "Do you now?"

I laugh. "I think so," I say.

Then I surprise myself.

I reach out and touch his hand.

His skin is warm, and it sends a delicious shiver through me.

He meets my eyes. "Real?" he asks in a low voice.

"Yes," I say.

Then we are quiet for a while.

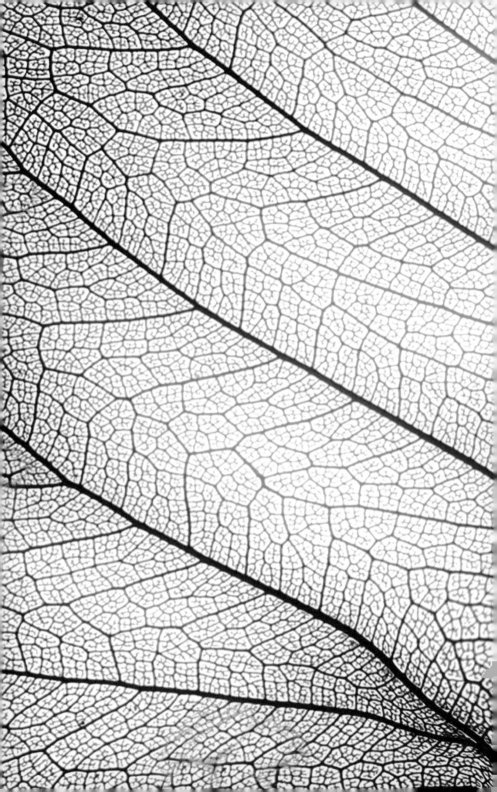

Lucy

Here is the story the willow queen tells me.

Once there was a kingdom. It was healthy and happy. The people who lived there were joyful. Things went wrong sometimes, but they solved their problems.

The queen of the kingdom had a baby, and the kingdom was full of joy.

It was a beautiful baby girl. They named her Hope.

Then the king died. It was terribly sad. Unexpected.

He had been a good king. He made the kingdom a good place to live. Everyone mourned him.

The queen didn't have time to cry. The kingdom needed a leader. She was the only one who could do it.

But some people in the kingdom—traitors—hated her. They wanted her power, or were jealous of it. They, with the help of the Ladybirds—outcasts who had left the kingdom generations ago—built up an army. And one night they came to the queen and they came into her rooms and they took the thing she loved the most. Her child. Her Hope. They stole the most valuable things the queen owned. The Dark Crown, and the royal seal.

They took the Dark Crown and buried it at the bottom of Black Lake. They tricked a human into diving down to hide it, because faeries can't swim. They knew the queen would never be able to retrieve the crown in its deep hiding spot.

And they took the baby and gave her to a witch, and they gave the witch a necklace. The royal seal was chained to it with faeriegold, which can't melt or burn or be broken by anyone but its owner. But the queen needed the royal seal and the Dark Crown. She needed them to restore the kingdom to power.

The queen, separated from her darling child, became so sad in her soul that she could barely move. The kingdom crumbled around her. The rest of the people, saddened by the sight of the queen's unhappiness, became unhappy themselves. Everyone knew that all the queen needed was the Dark Crown and the royal seal. And her daughter. Then the kingdom would bloom again, would become the place it was meant to be, the place it had been before the king left it.

That is the story she tells me. And I know without being told that some of it must be a lie.

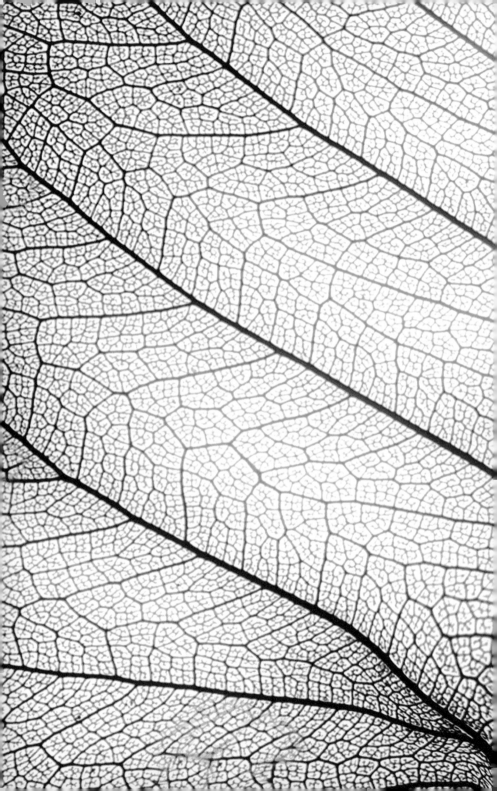

Soli

I'm starting to think we'll never reach the Black Lake.

Then, finally, we climb a small, grassy hill and pick our way through a stand of trees.

Beyond it is water.

"The Black Lake," Motherbird says. "And your crown is beneath the water."

Kheelan looks at me.

"Your crown?" he says, confusion darkening his face.

"That's right," Motherbird tells him. Then she looks at me and adds, "And you must be the one to retrieve it."

I look at the lake. It is black and churning.

I look back at Motherbird, but she is gone.

Kheelan shrugs. "The birds," he says. "They disappear."

I look at Black Lake again. "Am I supposed to just wear my clothes?" I ask.

"Do you have any choice?" Kheelan asks.

I open my backpack. Maybe there's a t-shirt in there, or a scarf, anything.

But no, there isn't.

Just a jar of fireflies.

I clasp the jar to my chest, wishing.

My wish is simple: *Help me.*

I open the jar and the lightning bugs swarm out.

I expect them to lead me somewhere, but instead they move together.

"They're weaving something," Kheelan says. He doesn't seem surprised.

After a moment, the fireflies disappear.

The jar is empty again.

And at my feet lies a thick, warm towel.

Without thinking, I dive deep into the water.

Lucy

Back in my cell.

I've lost track of what time it is. I keep thinking about the queen's story. The dead king. The witch who is my mother. The stolen baby. Who is Soli, or is me. I need to know the real story.

And then, as if an answer, the door to my cell opens and a faerie girl is shoved inside.

"I'll never tell!" she screams at the slamming door.

A key turns in a lock and we are alone.

The girl turns to me.

"Who are you?" she asks. She doesn't seem angry anymore, but her face is flushed.

"Um. I'm Lucy," I say.

She looks me up and down. "You're not from here," she says. "You're not one of us." Then she laughs.

"Why is that funny?" I ask.

The girl shrugs. "Because what does that mean, really," she says. "One of *us*. Who are *we*? You know?"

"The faeries?" I suggest.

"I suppose," she says. "But beyond that."

"What's your name?" I ask.

"Caro," she says. "Caro, the Betrayer."

"Who did you betray?" I ask.

"The kingdom, I suppose," she says. "The queen. You, if you're on her side."

"I don't even know what the sides are," I admit. "I don't trust the queen, but I don't know any other side of the story."

"You really aren't from around here, are you," Caro says, shaking her head. Her hair floats around her shoulders. It's light, like mine.

"No," I say, studying her. She's reminding me of my mother. How strange.

"You're human, right?" she asks.

"Yes."

"How did you get here?" she asks.

I tell her the story—or most of it, anyway. I don't know her, and I don't know who to trust. Even a girl who reminds me of my mother, of myself.

When I'm done telling the story of traveling into faerieground, Caro bends closer to me, looking at my eyes. "How do you feel?" she asks.

"Fine," I say. "Besides the fact that I'm trapped in some creepy castle and sleeping on the floor of a stone dungeon and my best friend is out there looking for a crown in a lake."

She laughs. "Fair enough," she says. "How long have you been here?"

"I don't know," I admit. I try to count hours. "Two days? Three?"

"Do you think Calandra will let you go soon?"

I shrug. "I hope so," I say. I rub my eyes, which feel

tired and sandy. "It's not exactly, like, a Holiday Inn." I laugh, but Caro's face stays blank, so I explain, "I don't want to stay here any longer than I have to."

"I can understand that," she says.

"Will you tell me the other side of the queen's story?" I ask. I bite my lip. She's my only chance to find out the truth.

Caro leans against the stone wall. Then she tells me.

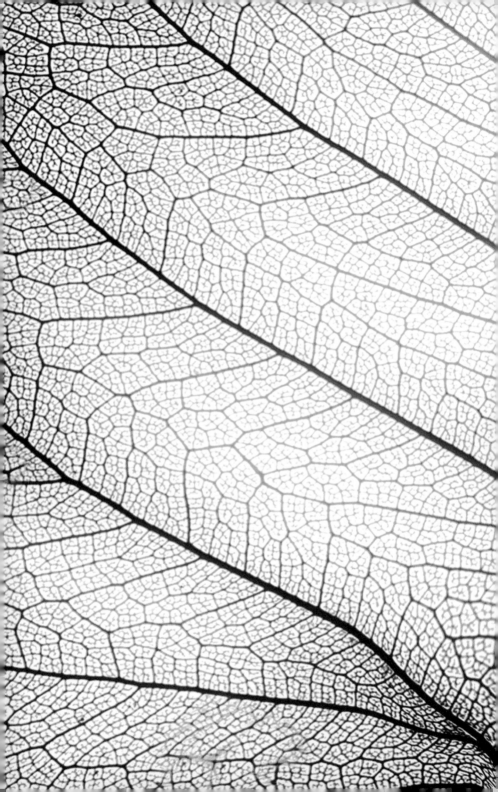

Soli

The water is cold. The water is hot.

The water is hard.

The water is soft.

I can't breathe. My arms and legs ache.

It's hard to get down to the bottom. It's hard to push through the water.

Beneath the water, far, far down, there is a metal box.

And inside the metal box there is a wooden box.

And inside the wooden box there is a velvet bag.

And inside the velvet bag there is a crown.

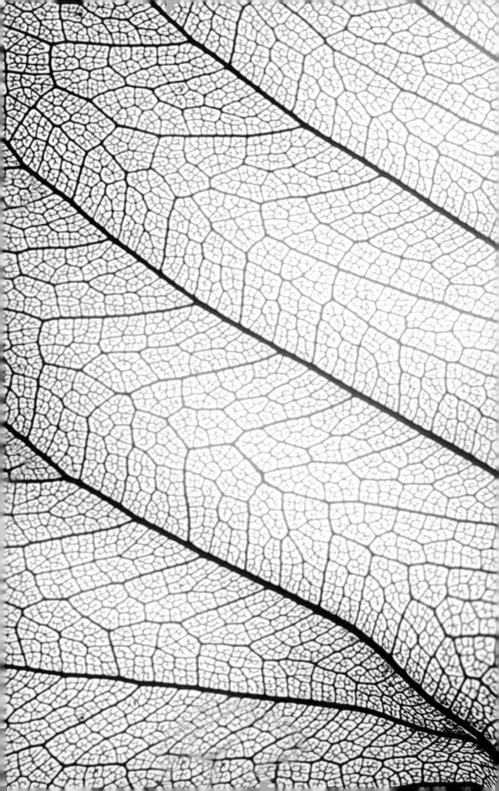

Lucy

Here is the story Caro tells me.

Once there was a kingdom built in a forest of willow trees. It was healthy and happy, though not perfect. Sometimes things went wrong. But problems were solved.

The king of the kingdom was lonely. Until he met a woman. Her name was Calandra. She was passing through the kingdom. No one knew where she was from or where she was going.

The willow king fell in love with her. They married. And right away, the kingdom changed.

Things began to go wrong. Problems couldn't be solved. The king seemed to disappear. The queen was cruel.

When the queen had a baby, there was hope in the kingdom. Perhaps the queen would learn to be kind. Perhaps the baby would bring life back to the kingdom.

Then the king died. He had never been sick, as far as anyone knew. There was no accident.

But that is a different story.

Once the king was gone, the queen was the only one in charge of the kingdom. Things went terribly wrong. She waged war on friends nearby. She took too much from everyone. People went hungry. People died. The people who tried to help her to see how things were falling apart—those people disappeared. Or they left. They joined a group of the oldest faeries, the Ladybirds, and they built an army.

And one night, the army put their plan into action.

They would save the kingdom, finally, by removing the princess.

So they came into Queen Calandra's rooms and took the baby and brought her out of the faerieground where she would be safe. They gave her to a woman who could protect her. And that woman found a family where the baby could hide. Then the only thing keeping the queen in power were the royal emblems. The Dark Crown, and the royal seal. They took the crown and sank it at the bottom of Black Lake. And they gave the seal to the woman protecting the baby. It would keep the baby safer. It was her birthright. It did not belong to the queen.

After that, the queen stayed in power. The Ladybirds and their army had done all they could. The faeries left in the kingdom needed to overthrow the queen, and to do that, they needed the princess. And the princess was just a baby. They needed to wait.

But the queen wanted the baby back. She knew that in order to stay in power, she needed to get her daughter on her side. Or the queen needed to kill her.

The kingdom crumbled around the willow queen, but she was still in control.

And once the princess returned, the queen would have all the power there was. She would retrieve the crown and the seal.

Everything would be in place.

So Queen Calandra waited. She waited for the daughter to get old enough to be angry.

This is the story Caro tells me. This time I believe each word.

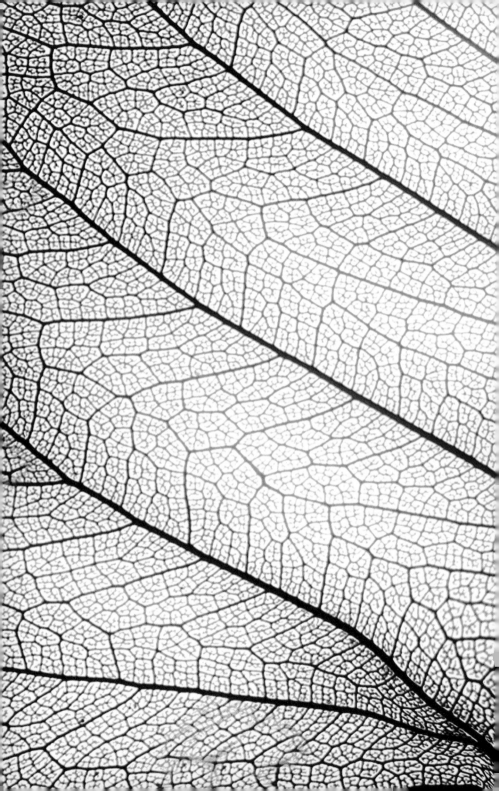

Soli

I am soaking wet when I climb out of the water.

Kheelan wraps my firefly towel around me.

He holds me close.

The towel dries me quickly and then dissolves.

"We should hurry," Kheelan says, looking up at the sky.

The light is fading. We only have until tomorrow morning at sunrise.

"Thank you," I say.

He smiles. "For what?" he asks.

"For helping me. For coming along."

He reaches out and smoothes my hair. "Of course, princess," he says.

Then he kisses me.

Then we run.

Lucy

"The queen's story was different," I tell Caro.

"Of course it was," Caro says. She's dug a bit of chocolate out of her pocket, and we're sharing it. "That's how she works."

"I have a question," I admit, breaking off a tiny square of the sweet, dark bar. "Why'd they put the crown under the lake? She said it was because faeries couldn't swim. Is that true?"

Caro laughs, a short, angry laugh. "No," she says. "It

isn't true. You have to have a little faerie blood to enter the Black Lake."

I stop eating. I look at her. "What?" I ask.

"You have to have faerie blood. Otherwise the lake drowns you."

"I don't understand," I say.

"The queen," she explains. "She's not faerie. She's human. That's why she can't leave. Because she'd never be able to return. That's why they hid the crown. Because it was the only thing giving her power."

"Then why isn't she just overthrown?" I ask, confused.

Caro shrugs, swallows the last bite of chocolate. "She's tricked everyone," she says. "They're under her spell. She's a witch."

"She said my mother was a witch," I mutter.

Caro's head snaps up. "Your mother knows her?" she asks.

"I guess so," I say. "That's what my mom told me, anyway."

"What's her name?"

"Andria," I say.

Caro shakes her head. "I don't know the name," she says. "But that doesn't mean it's not true, what your mother said. How does she know Queen Calandra?"

I trace my finger through the dust on the stone floor. "My mother doesn't really talk about it. She told me once, a long time ago, that she angered the queen. And the queen said that they gave the baby to my mother. So I guess that's how she made the queen mad."

"What did your mother do with the baby?" Caro asks.

I shrug. "I don't know," I say. "I assumed that part of the story wasn't true."

Caro stands, her face a picture of shock. "No. I think it is true," she says. "You're the baby. You're Hope. You're the princess."

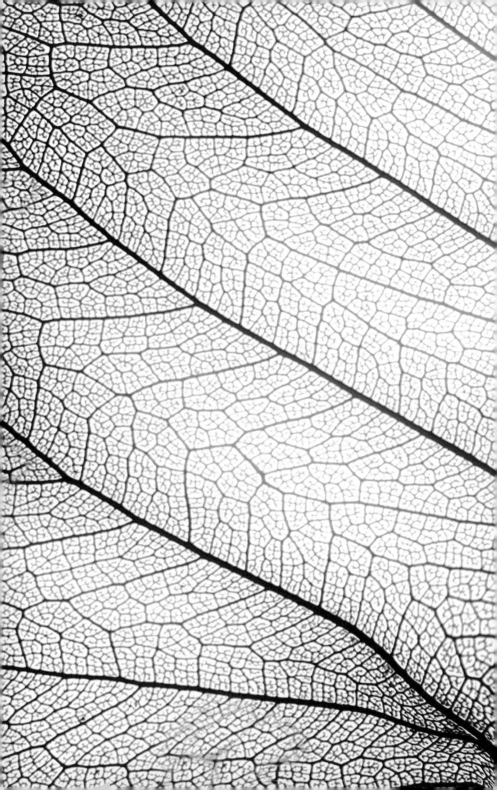

Soli

Kheelan and I run.

The whole time we run, a red-hot rose blooms in my chest.

Its roots spread into my arms and legs.

The feeling of Kheelan's lips on mine.

Soon, the palace rises up in front of us. It is almost dawn.

Guards find us as soon as we enter the palace grounds.
They snap us into chains and lead us to the throne room.

The queen sweeps in, eyes red.
She looks tired.
She looks angry.

She stares at me. "Where is it?" she asks.

Not asks.
Demands.

The chains binding my arms disappear.
The queen crosses her arms.

"Give me the crown," she says. "Now. Then you can
see your friend."

I open my backpack. The velvet bag is inside.
"Wait," Kheelan whispers. "Make sure you get what
you want first."

I zip up my bag again. "Where is Lucy?" I ask.

"Give me the crown," the queen says.

I am afraid, but I try not to show it.

The warmth of Kheelan's body next to mine gives me strength.

Or maybe it's my own strength.

"No," I say. The chains snap back onto my wrists.

"No?" the queen roars. "No?"

"No," I say again, my voice shaking. "Bring me my friend. Bring Lucy here."

Queen Calandra rolls her eyes. "Fine," she says. She points at one of the guards and says, "Bring me the girl."

The guard looks at me quickly, and I swear he winks. Then he's gone.

Queen Calandra taps her foot while we wait. "I suppose you saw the crazy loons," she says to Kheelan. "I'm sure they filled your heads with more nonsense."

Kheelan stands straight. "Not nonsense," he says. "But they filled our heads, yes. They led us to the lake. They told Soli what she was looking for and they told her who it belongs to."

Then the queen's eyes narrow.
She looks afraid. But she shakes it off.

"So you dove down into Black Lake," she says to me. "Why aren't your clothes wet?"
I look down at myself. "I had a towel," I say.

The queen laughs. "A towel. You thought to bring a towel."
I shake my head.
But Kheelan speaks. "She didn't bring it," he says. "It was given to her."

The queen opens her mouth, but before she can speak, the door to the throne room is thrown open.

A guard leads Lucy inside.

Lucy

"Lucy!" Soli screams. Though we're both in chains, we run to each other and try to hug. I'm so happy to see her. I'm so grateful that she found me.

But now I'm afraid. If I am the willow queen's daughter, like Caro thinks I am, what happens next? Do I have to stay here? Will she treat me better once she discovers who I am?

The story makes sense.

I was given to my mother for safekeeping. That

explains why I've always felt like my mother didn't truly love me. That she cared more about Soli.

But I can't keep thinking about it. Soli is crying into my hair. "I'm here," I whisper. "Don't worry. I'll get you out of here."

Hands rip us apart. "Now give me the crown," Queen Calandra—my mother?—says, towering above us.

Soli glances at Kheelan. Then she takes my hand. "No," she says. "It belongs to me."

And she reaches into her backpack, pulls out a crown, and places it on her head.

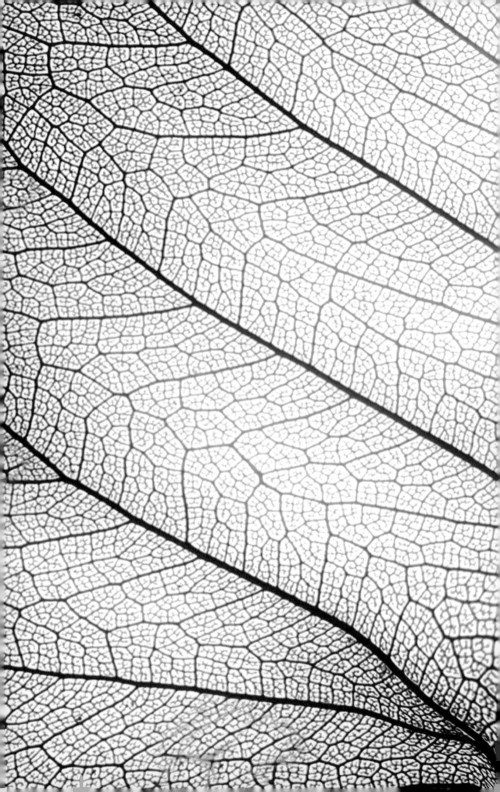

Soli

At first, the queen looks shocked.

Then she laughs.

"You'll need more than just that dirty old crown," she says. "It's worthless on its own, daughter."

Daughter.

Lucy gasps. "Of course," she whispers. "Of course."

"Of course what?" I ask.

She laughs lightly. "Of course it isn't me," she says. "Never mind. I thought—never mind."

"Did you know?" I ask. "About me?"
Lucy shakes her head.

"The crown!" the queen roars.

"Stop yelling," Kheelan says.
A guard shoves him backward.

"Give it to me now," the queen says now, her voice quiet, cold. "There's no point in you having it. It's worthless. It's junk. It's only worth something to me. Sentimental value."

"I don't believe her," Lucy whispers.

Neither do I.

I take off the crown, turn it around in my hands. Now I can look at it in the light for the first time.

On one side, there's a small hole.

As if something was there and then broken from it in a perfect circle.

The size of the pendant Andria gave me.

Then I know what to do.

Lucy

Soli reaches into her shirt and pulls out my mother's necklace.

She rips the chain from her throat, breaking it. Then she places the pendant into a hole on the side of the crown.

She places the crown on top of her own head. Wings bud from her back. Our chains melt.

Kheelan laughs. "Now you're you," he says. "Welcome home."

A guard whispers, "Princess."

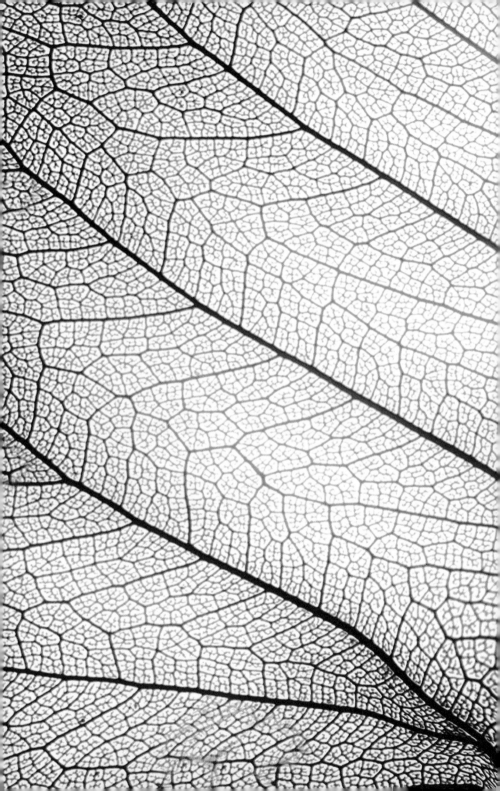

31

Soli

I look my mother in the eye, but she can't meet my gaze.

The guards kneel. Kheelan kneels.

"Who are you?" I ask.

Calandra looks down.

"I'm the queen," she says, but now her voice is the one that shakes.

"Remove the glamour," Kheelan whispers. "Just wish it away."

"Don't," Calandra says. She's begging. "You don't know what you're doing."

"I wish to remove the glamour on this woman," I say.

Her wings fall away.

The queen moans.

She's just a normal woman now, getting old, all alone.

Then I look at Lucy and say, "I wish to send my friend—"

"No!" Lucy yells.

"You have to go home, Lucy," I say. "Your mom is so worried."

"What about you?" Lucy asks. "What will you do?"

I look around.

The castle is crumbling.

The people who live here are afraid.

The queen—my mother—is crying.

The guards are waiting.

And Kheelan still kneels before me.

He stands and takes my hand. "There's work to be done here," he says.

I know he's right.

The Dark Crown is heavy on my head.

The wings are light on my back.

"I have to stay," I tell Lucy.

"Then I will stay too," says Lucy. "I'll help you." Tears fall from her eyes.

"We should ask your mom," I say, like I've said a million times before—about dinners, playtimes, movies, sleepovers.

I picture telling Andria—what?

That I'm a faerie princess?

That I need Lucy to help me save my kingdom?

Will she believe me?

What do I do next?

Lucy takes my hand.

"We'll ask my mom," she says. "And then I'll help you."

We have always been together, Lucy and I.

She was the brave one.

I was the fearful one.

Not anymore.

Together, we step back through the willow queen's gate.

Beth & Kay

Kay Fraser and *Beth Bracken* are a designer-editor team in Minnesota.

Kay is from Buenos Aires. She left home at eighteen and moved to North Dakota—basically the exact opposite of Argentina. These days, she designs books, writes, makes tea for her husband, and drives her daughters to their dance lessons.

Beth lives in a light-filled house with her husband and their son, Sam. She spends her time editing books, reading, daydreaming, and rearranging her furniture.

Kay and Beth both love dark chocolate, Buffy, and tea.

Odessa

Odessa Sawyer is an illustrator from Santa Fe, New Mexico. She works mainly in digital mixed media, utilizing digital painting, photography, and traditional pen and ink.

Odessa's work has graced the book covers of many top publishing houses, and she has also done work for various film and television projects, posters, and album covers.

Highly influenced by fantasy, fairy tales, fashion, and classic horror, Odessa's work celebrates a whimsical, dreamy, and vibrant quality.

Discover

Turn the page for Chapter 1 of the next book in the

Faerieground cycle—coming soon!

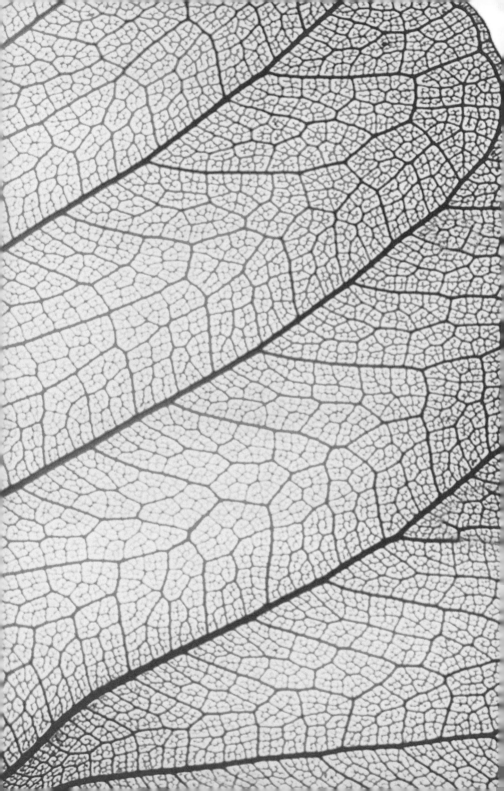

1

Soli

I can't stop thinking about my other mother.

My real mother, my mom, the one who adopted me. I don't know the whole story, of course. There's so much left to learn.

How did Andria explain me to her?
How did she convince her?

How much does she know?

Does she love me?

She must love me.

She and my father both must love me.

Did they know I would leave them one day?

Do they know who I am, who I would become?

Kheelan, who knows these woods so well, is leading Lucy and me to the clearing where the big willow tree stands in the middle of the forest.

The door.

The path home.

The way I came in, the way I'll return.

My wings, once light, are heavy on my back.

We are quiet. I can hear the creek nearby, and I know that in the woods, Calandra's armies follow us.

Every few steps, a twig snaps, a leaf rustles.

Kheelan shoots me a glance, and I nod.

Yes, I heard it. He nods back. We both heard the noise, and we both know what it means.

I'm surprised, but not surprised. He and I can talk without saying a word.

We are in real danger, I understand. We aren't being pursued; we're being tracked. And when Lucy and I leave, Kheelan will still be here, and he'll still be in danger.

They are angry. Whoever Calandra's people are, they're angry.

I stripped the queen—my real mother—of her powers.

Of course her armies are angry. I should have known they would be.

There is a battle ahead of us, I know that now.

But before the battle can begin, I have things to do at home.

So we trudge on, slowly, softly through the woods.

Suddenly I notice that Kheelan is holding my hand.

Above us, a crow cries.

Lucy

Her wings! I can't stop staring at them.

As Soli and Kheelan lead me through the woods, I think about what I've learned in the last few hours.

Soli is a princess. Her mother is a human woman who was a cruel tyrant in the faerie kingdom. We're going home to tell my mother that I need to return to the faerieground and fight. We're going home to tell Soli's parents what we know.

Soli is a princess, a faerie princess.

Also, she's totally holding hands with Kheelan.

When we get to the big old tree in the middle of the woods, we stop. Soli shifts her body, stretching her arms. Her wings shimmer in the light streaming through the trees.

She smiles when she sees me looking at them. "I'm never going to get used to these," she says.

"Me either," I say, and just like that I can stop worrying about things changing: we are just Soli and Lucy again, best friends.

Kheelan pushes leaves away from the tree's roots. "Do you know what to do?" he asks.

I'm used to being the leader, the one in charge, the one with the plan, so I say, "No."

But he's not looking at me. Of course he isn't. He's looking at Soli.

Soli takes off her crown and hands it to Kheelan. She closes her eyes for a moment, and her wings disappear: not gone, I know, but hidden.

I look at the crown. "Could I—could I hold it?" I ask. "

Kheelan passes it to me. It's still warm from resting on Soli's head.

It doesn't look like much, this crown. Almost like a bundle of twigs. It's very old, and somehow feels brittle and strong at the same time. I think about the fact that it sat on Calandra's head for so long, and that makes me shiver.

Kheelan clears his throat, and I look up. "Sorry," I mutter, and hand the crown back to him.

"That's okay," Soli says. "But we do have to go now."

It's so strange, I think, how quickly my friend has become brave.

"It must be strange," Kheelan says, looking at me. For a second I think he's read my mind. Then he says, "To discover that your friend is a princess, and has been all along, without you knowing it."

Soli frowns. "I'm the same," she says. "And since Lucy is more like my sister, it's almost as if we're both princesses."

I laugh, but it feels flat and false.

"I didn't mean—" Kheelan begins, but I stop him.

"I know," I say. "And yes. It is strange."

"I have the feeling it isn't the last strange thing you'll see here," he tells me.

"But first, back home," Soli says.

She steps forward and kneels down. She puts a palm on a root and turns to look up at Kheelan. They stretch their hands to touch.

"I'll be back soon," she says.

"I know," he says. "Be safe, but hurry. There's so much to do, and so much still to explain. Come back as soon as you can."

"I will," she says, and then takes my hand, and then we are gone.